The Chilean Spring

Fernando Alegría
Translated by Stephen Fredman

LATIN AMERICAN LITERARY REVIEW PRESS
SERIES: DISCOVERIES
PITTSBURGH, PENNSYLVANIA 1980

The Latin American Literary Review publishes Latin American creative writing under the series title *Discoveries*, and critical works under the series title *Explorations*.

Spanish Edition Copyright © 1975 by Fernando Alegría.
English Translation Copyright © 1980 by
Fernando Alegría and Stephen Fredman.

No part of this book may be reproduced by any means, including information storage and retrieval or photocopying except for short excerpts quoted in critical articles, without the written permission of the publisher.

Library of Congress Cataloging in Publication
Number: 79-91641

ISBN 0-935480-01-3, Cloth
0-935480-00-5, Paper

This project is partially supported by a grant from the National Endowment for the Arts in Washington, D.C., a Federal agency.

We wish to thank David Smith and Marcelo Montesino for their work translating an earlier version of this book. —F.A. and S.F.

The Chilean Spring can be ordered directly from the publisher, Latin American Literary Review Press,
P.O. Box 8316, Pittsburgh, Pennsylvania 15218
for $7.95 plus 80¢ postage and handling.

Cover photo taken inside National Stadium, Santiago, 1973, by Cristián.

PREFACE

No sooner had the Battle of Santiago begun on September 11, 1973, than we who are speaking here got together as quickly as possible and proceeded to bang out our testimony. I say "bang" because our voices mingled with the sound of rifles, machine guns and explosives, and because each of us had a moment of reckoning, whether to load or unload our weapons. Some of us, as soldiers, ran to our barracks (regiments, police stations, war academies, ships, air fields), and others, being students, went to our combat stations (universities and schools); the rest of us, workers, laborers and squatters, entrenched ourselves in the industrial belts. Our President, Salvador Allende, gathered his personal guard about him in the palace of La Moneda and closed the colonial doors, barring entrance to the trucks, tanks, ambulances and helicopters.

People of a more pacific cast were at a loss as to how to behave: more than one went out in the street and found the bullets of military patrols or police; others died while they peered through the half-opened shutters of their homes; others filled the churches and, when necessary, prayed and helped to load the dead. The firemen sprayed huge sheets of water on the burning roofs of La Moneda, and later, about four o'clock, formed a column of smoke and leather, rubber and soot, and carried the President out on a stretcher, covering him with a somber-toned Bolivian rug. Most people, however, stayed at home, thinking, using the telephone, consecrating their own dead, listening for the knock of the search parties and book burners and the honking of buses, as on the days of important soccer games, accelerating toward the Stadium.

*

I knew Salvador Allende in the Forties, when he was already a doctor and a well-known political figure. I accompanied him as a supporter during his presidential campaigns of 1964 and 1970.

Why? For a very simple reason: I have always been convinced—now more than ever—of the sincerity, the importance and the depth of Allende's humanist position. As a Socialist, he was devoted to improving the lot of the exploited and the oppressed. He believed that it was still possible to effect a peaceful revolution within the constitutional framework under which the Chilean nation had governed itself for more than a hundred and fifty years.

In a country where most of the arable land was in the hands of a powerful minority, where "Chile's Salary" (copper) was owned by multinationals guilty of scandalously excessive profits, Allende came to power with a program to nationalize the copper industry and accelerate agrarian reform. He promoted legislation guaranteeing the rights of women and minorities and brought food and medical attention to the children of a country with one of the highest infant mortality rates in the world.

The multinationals and their allies within the Chilean oligarchy unleashed a virulent policy of economic destabilization and terrorism.

On September 11, 1973, the armed forces rebelled against the constitutional government of Salvador Allende. For a period of twelve hours, Allende and a small group of men and women resisted the brutal onslaught of the Air Force, tanks and infantry. "Hawk Hunter" jets demolished the presidential palace of La Moneda with powerful missiles. After leading his two daughters and the other women fighting alongside him to safety, President Allende died in battle.

A short time before his death, Allende said, "I have faith in Chile and in its destiny. This gray and bitter moment, when treason is in the ascendant, will be overcome in turn by Chileans to follow. Know that sooner rather than later, the grand avenues will once more open wide to welcome the just men who will walk through them and build a new society."

I also knew Cristián the photographer personally. The few pages of his notebook and his letters, which appear at the beginning of our story, I received directly from his mother.

*

A poor people, but stoic; a country of wind and sky, with snow to survive on, a deep ocean to hear our confessions, felled trees that sprout anew, deadly forests of rain and ferns and petrified evergreens, an Easter Island and a Land of Fire, Chile, we believe in it and we have loved it the way a son is loved whom nobody understands, few appreciate, and everyone forgets. And the son grows up from adolescence to manhood, acquires the voice of Pablo Neruda, and suddenly the world takes heed.

*Cristián's
Notebook and Letters*

The pages of this diary and the accompanying letters are transcribed verbatim as they were written by Cristián Montealegre, a young photographer shot in Santiago, Chile, by a military detachment. There exists an official report, signed and sealed by the authorities, which makes no reference to an execution but rather to shots resulting from an "attempt to flee."

NOTEBOOK

AUGUST 30, 1973

I have so much to write about. That's why I bought this notebook, which I would rather not call a diary.

It doesn't matter where I start. Maybe on the flight home on July 2. The plane was flying low and the day was coming to an end. The vast deserts and mountain ranges looked empty and sterile. When I was a boy they seemed mysterious, peaceful, majestic. And I was crying, tears streaming down my face, because I didn't know where I was going or where I was coming from. I looked out the window so my sons wouldn't see me.

SEPTEMBER 1, 1973

It seems significant that, in my desire to communicate, I am writing here instead of scribbling letters. I write here feeling my thoughts aren't sinking to the bottom of the ocean.

My sacrifices have been so useless. I'm in conflict and I suffer now because I've followed certain ideals and on the way I've had to destroy so many people. Nevertheless, I still long for profound human contact.

My future is uncertain. I'm ready for whatever happens. I'll risk it all. Nobody needs me anymore. There are the boys, sure, but it's not easy for me to reach them.

On the plane I was thinking I'm not young any more. There was no challenge for me in the dangerous switch to a new life. I am not the kind of man to make a courageous adventure out of life and overcome circumstances; nor am I young, because I can't see into the future. Not a man at all, since my past escapes me. My life was slipping away and I saw that soon I would be completely alone, just as if I were facing death itself.

When we landed I didn't feel anything beginning; something was ending. But I didn't know what that something was. An intuition. I didn't understand what was waiting for me. It was like seeing a new me in the future. A better or worse one, I don't know. I feel like a small stone rolling along, almost stopping, going on, barely moving at all these last two months. It hits another one. At optimistic moments I see in my new self an avalanche that perhaps alters the ground. I feel as if there is some seed left in me, though I have planted twice without success—that it's still here like some great treasure I have to offer.

SEPTEMBER 10, 1973

What imperceptible changes take place in us without our knowing it. Like walking: we choose a path, and the path makes us walk, as Antonio Machado says. The path changes, we change, perhaps we see the same thing from a different angle. Everything is a mixture of ourselves and luck. We put out the ideas, the attitude and the spirit. Luck dictates the surroundings. The world is the body and we are the soul.

SEPTEMBER 11, 1973

The world has collapsed around me. Civil war. I'll describe the events. 10:00 AM. The shooting started at La Moneda Palace. I was two blocks away. Snipers kill and wound while I shoot pictures. In my building the soldiers take away my film. Now there are snipers everywhere. We see the bombing of La Moneda.

UP TO THE 18TH

Battle and 500 dead in Puente Alto, Cousiño Park, the SUMAR factory, Lo Hermida, La Legua, Copiapo and San Borja. 400 dead at Sumar (after surrendering). 1700 dead in La Legua, squatters bombed from the air. Two truckloads of soldiers blown up. 27 executed 200 meters from here.

SEPTEMBER 19, 1973

Some power lines were blown up just a few blocks away from my brother Marcelo. 7 executed in Ñuñoa. 42 executed in Copiapo. People shot for alleged involvement in black market at Central Station. Miristas with machine guns in the barrios. A friend of Mari's, a communist woman, dead, leaving behind a month-old baby (Chile Stadium).

LETTERS

SEPTEMBER 11, 1973

On this terrible day, the eleventh of September, gunfire and corpses outside—on a day that will be remembered for a long time—exhausted, I try to write you and communicate something of what happened.

It all started at 8:30. By coincidence Marcelo came by to see me. I had just come back from La Moneda. We set out together around 9:30, and about 10:00 we were near the Cathedral when the tanks began arriving, some 15 of them plus jeeps. Two blocks from La Moneda, Marcelo says to me: "In case of shooting we hit the ground," just about the time the snipers opened fire on the people in the Alameda. I was behind a newsstand taking pictures of people running and throwing themselves to the ground. Through the camera, while taking a shot, I watch a man fall. Some kids try to help him, but there is nothing they can do. An ambulance comes, but when they see he's dead, they leave. Then there are bullets everywhere. But in La Moneda there is an all out *battle. What with tanks, machine gun fire and small arms, in 20 minutes there must have been no one left. The noise was unbelievable. Suddenly, they shoot from behind. In the midst of this Marcelo disappeared. I ran up and down side streets to see if I could find him. When I got home they were searching the building. There was nothing I could do. They took away my camera and exposed my film. They gave me back my camera and left. I couldn't go to Plaza Baquedano because there were soldiers everywhere. I had to hide in this building for I don't know how long. The snipers have shot up all these buildings. A bullet barely missed a girl on this floor. We watched the shooting all day. Next door at the School of Pharmacology there was a huge battle with bazookas, resulting in great destruction and heavy casualties.*

SEPTEMBER 12 AND 13, 1973

The urban guerilla war goes on. We woke up to the sound of automatic rifles and windows breaking in the building. Between yesterday and today five apartments have been riddled with bullets, luckily without harming anyone. The last incident was ten minutes ago, four floors down. The guerillas and the army are shooting it out. There are shots coming from here, too. They've even machine-gunned helicopters. There could be a thousand dead, nobody knows. A lot of bodies have been seen in the Metro ditches. Yesterday and today I saw battles in the Plaza Baquedano and Plaza Bulnes. This morning, in a downtown building, they riddled four floors for ten minutes. Nobody could have survived.

It is now 4:30 PM. The ultimatum for the guerillas to surrender has expired. We are waiting. Bombers have passed over us. The same ones that bombed the barrios and the factories. They are capable of blowing up all these buildings. Although I'm ready for anything, nothing really matters anymore. Not a minute goes by without the sound of shooting. Father and some others were on the first floor and they got shot at by machine guns. There isn't much re-

sistance in the hospital. From here I can watch the wounded brought in to San Borja. We're right in the middle of everything. They say Allende committed suicide after requesting an escort to surrender. It sounds very suspicious. It makes sense that our military dictators would want him dead so there would be no danger of him returning. That's why, even after that, they leveled La Moneda and his home at Tomás Moro. They don't realize that during these few days they have made hundreds of martyrs, a giant out of Allende, and thousands of new sympathizers. They took away our freedom and ignorant fools rejoice, not knowing if we'll ever get it back. Where will they go when they want justice? The guerillas are still fighting and they'll keep on, perhaps with more strength, since the cause itself and the hatred for those who steal power with violence will surely grow and find expression. Chile doesn't know what a dictatorship is. If they don't turn over the power soon the country will be permanently divided. Chile blew apart yesterday. The military will never be able to restrain what it has unleashed. They don't know what they're doing. Both sides are engaged in a fratricidal struggle that will not end for a generation. There won't be thousands of dead like yesterday and today, but the country will bleed out slowly like Ireland or Vietnam or the Middle East.

It may be a good thing I was here and witnessed this. From the outside, and especially now with no freedom, no one will know how it really was. There was a destiny in my coming to Chile, although what it was is still unclear. It's developing. Tanks are shooting near here. It seems like downtown. Dynamite blew up two truckloads of soldiers. I don't know what else to say. It makes me sad to be around people who celebrate all this and vent their hatred even on those who died. I don't want to be infected. I'm afraid of willing someone's death. I don't want to think of myself with either cause, both inconclusive. Perhaps this defines everything: Chile is now a country without a solution.

The truth is that although I have much to say and relate, restlessness won't let me write. Marcelo, while trying to walk to Plaza Baquedano, was stopped and had to return. I spoke to him and he's okay. Only those who live downtown and in San Borja, Central Station and around there are pinned down by the bullets from the snipers and the army. Even now, September 13, with people going back to work at noon, you can still hear the shooting. The leftists will sow panic and want to paralyze the country with their death tactics, as the previous opposition did. God save us from both sides. We have no news. Only from Argentina, by shortwave, did we hear of Allende's death. Now that people are in communication they will hear by word of mouth the tales of agony and death in this civil war. For the first time I'm ashamed of Chile: because I'm not used to being censored, because we won't be able to work in freedom and because hatred is here in massive doses.

I will write later and tell you my plans. The fighting continues, everything is so confused. Last night, downstairs, they caught 23 leftists and apparently executed them on the spot. The killing thrives on both sides. We will continue to be isolated. We were told not to drink the water because it might be poisoned.

SEPTEMBER 14, 1973

I'll enumerate for you the new developments according to people who saw them firsthand, including me:

1. In Puente Alto they had to hose down the plaza four times because of the bloodstains. There was an awful slaughter there.

2. In Lo Hermida they hung two dead Carabineros from some beams. When the patrols arrived, they ordered all the women and children to leave, saying in 15 minutes they would machinegun everything. The resistance leaders did not allow anyone to leave. In 15 minutes they killed everyone there, men, women and children.

3. In Cousiño Park there was a huge battle. They raked the Popular Unity from the air. A lady who lives nearby said there were hundreds of dead, bodies everywhere you looked.

4. From the SUMAR factory, after the resistance, they took off bodies by the truckload directly to the crematorium.

5. Yesterday I heard two tremendous explosions near here. Two truckloads of soldiers were blown up with sticks of dynamite thrown from a building.

6. Just now, a few minutes ago, bullets were going by a few feet from my window. Right in front of me I could see them ricochet off the other building. The soldiers were firing from an apartment above. They shot the door down. They're still at it today.

SEPTEMBER 15, 1973

1. Shooting night and day. They shot up two houses in Bustamante. Shots near Lucha's window.

2. I was at Mauricio's. Last night they saw two neighbors of theirs executed, two kids who were outside after 9:00 PM. When they spotted the Carabineros they went towards them with their hands in the air. The Carabineros made them cross the street, put their hands up against the wall, said they were going to shoot them and opened fire while their parents watched from the window. They didn't allow anyone near until 10:00 AM the next morning. As I went by I saw the blood and bulletholes all over the wall. These last few days ten people died on that block. Mauricio is very worried because he has two pistols. If they search these apartments, as they have promised to do, they'll show less mercy than to those who break the curfew. He also has machine gun bullets. My father too has a gun which we hid. If you turn it in, you are arrested and shot.

3. Today they carted off four people from this building. A Uruguayan girl who has been scared to death since Tuesday, and whose only sin was to sympathize with the Left. They also arrested some leftists from across the hall, accused of "hoarding" (which can mean having more than one can of milk).

4. Marcelo tells us that in his neighborhood people

have been shot for charging black market prices.

5. In the barrios fifteen-year-old kids go out with submachine guns to kill soldiers.

SEPTEMBER 16, 1973

1. They killed a friend of Luz María who has a one-month-old baby. She was a communist activist (33 years old).
2. A Carabinero station in Las Tranqueras was attacked. Thirty leftists. Now they are launching offensives.
3. While we were guarding the building last night four Carabineros came over and told us stories. How the leftists have killed cops, hanging them, cutting off their balls. They told us some of them almost blew up the emergency hospital with the furnaces going full blast, that they've blown up bridges, roads, towers, etc. One of them dressed as a Carabinero colonel drove around in an ambulance and killed nine soldiers before they got him. The Carabineros took four days to take over the Burger plant.

SEPTEMBER 19, 1973

They blew up the street lights. Not so much shooting lately and almost none when people go out. A girl was telling us yesterday about forty-three workers she saw executed in Copiapo. Another friend saw seven bodies with their hands still tied behind their backs in the Cultural Center of Ñuñoa. A Frenchman, who has been in Chile Stadium where most have been killed, says it's terrible. The bullets were bouncing off the roof down at the people. A man asked to go to the bathroom, a Carabinero smashed his face, he bled to death. Another one, who couldn't breathe with his ribs broken, was forced to stand up to get knocked down again. Almost no one gets out of there.

The streets are nearly empty. Everyone looks at everyone else with distrust. A lot of people are still being arrested. No one is safe, neither Americans or journalists or the ambulances which are fired on by both sides.

There's no point in going on because it would take a book and it's too depressing. We have good photographs already, but plenty of work for later. Don't even think of coming. We'll be leaving in a couple of months. By then we'll know more about the future. Because I won't feel easy leaving the children in danger. I'll write you everything that happens. Get those credentials for us so we won't be arrested.

Pray for Chile.

NOTEBOOK

SEPTEMBER 23, 1973

At this moment in my life I see death everywhere. Pablo Neruda died today. By coincidence I spent the afternoon at the General Cemetery listening to the macabre stories of truckloads of unidentified bodies being brought to the crematorium. There was a truck from the National Stadium, which I visited a couple of days ago with the reporters. Marcelo was arrested but released. Public executions on suspicion, the bodies thrown into the river. Life is cheap in Chile. Truckloads of bodies, thousands dead and arrested. I pause for a while wondering what I want to say. I question myself and think how this has changed me and my life. Evidently, I'm assimilating so much at once—none of it positive—that it's an effort to recognize myself. I'm lost in all of this. I am a nonentity. I have no pride. But neither am I humble. I have no desire to cope with these events which are destroying me. I've suffered the danger, the hatred, the ignorance, the violence and the brutality of a civil war. Now I have to face the possibility of more waiting, more repression, the same loneliness, the same problems, without the desire or the energy to seek new horizons. For what? For whom? I don't enjoy being alone. I wish I did, because I'd go forget the world in a cabin and live out my life like that.

Soon it will be spring. I'll be able to leave, and hopefully I'll have found a little God-given energy to go to Europe, get a job, start all over again, one more time. Maybe all this will be behind me. But now, even my desires—to write this, for example—are fleeting.

That about sums it up.

OCTOBER 10, 1973

God . . . though each one of us in this world is born, lives and dies, the beginning and the end we never taste firsthand. Life is all that's left. But, beneath it all waits that loneliness, which means, perhaps, being out of communion with God. These days I cry at the drop of a hat. Am more easily unburdened. Now I must find myself. Life is a contradiction, an ongoing dilemma. We're the only ones who count.

Father is just as reserved, although he seems to be happy to have me here (I don't see much of him). My aunts complain, but secretly enjoy the hardships which give more life to their lives. Uncle Claudio has cancer of the prostate, but father says he'll be all right. I gave some blood for him.

My present situation gives my brother a chance to see me in a different light, but sometimes I seem too fragile and other times he considers me a clumsy fool.

*The Gospel
According to Cristián*

It seemed to me we had all lost our way: a young father, a crazy young woman, two children as shepherds or two stars in a world without lambs—only wolves—missing a sky; but also that childless father who buries his head between his shoulders and sees his reflection in the desert and in the sudden whirlwind of sand swaddling the tail of an airplane. Where are we coming from, if not from the same mystery out there, that great loneliness leaning like a bird on our metal wings and that same towering melancholy of mountains lowering like a screen in the Atacama sunset?

Did the man and woman in flight ever find the right road? They drink with good cheer and talk without listening, cross over mountains without recognizing each other, busy with the years that go by and others on their way, searching heedlessly for (lacking the will or the desire to find) themselves: a man and a woman thrown into a bottomless postal sack, parcels with no name or address or postage, stirring life about with a finger in a glass full of ice.

Maybe we'll find out the answer when we get there. But I've been there many times and the trip and the arrival are always the same: a gloomy wait, anxiety before the confrontation, a sad defeat. All I can see are faces reflected in dark glasses, scenes on an old porch lit with yellow bulbs, second-hand people I knew and loved who forgot me. I can't even find enemies who could help me figure what's been done and what's left to do. A simple indifference surrounds me and I slip inside it as if I'd ceased to exist.

Naturally I have the right to start over again, and, in what little night we have left, improvise some kind of peace with myself, perhaps even an arrangement—a kind of gentleman's agreement—with some God. Ah! if I could only go from supply to demand! Starting all over again is a matter of knowing who You are when I talk to You, and that there is no need for words, since You and I walk down the street maintaining a discreet distance, and that it's enough to nod agreement frowning slightly, or pursing the lips, to know our destiny, Yours and mine. As for Luz María and the children, something else awaits them.

To start all over again is to know for certain if this plane will make it, whether it will land on the chalk circle assigned to it, and if it can stay there; if the runway, the building, the people stretching out their arms on the roof, can be trusted or if it's all a trick; if the customs agents really see me and if their stamp is a secret signal to the police expecting me outside.

I ought to write first about my father, who never bothers me; in fact, he allows me to make my peace with something which may have nothing to do with him. Whatever was keeping us apart has been overcome. There are no doubts or suspicions between us. We are united by a certain calm consciousness of what we won't ever be, neither he nor I. It's possible my case is not completely clear to him. If my father were keeping this journal, he would leave a lot of empty pages, or he would fill it with pious reflections about the present and the future of the country. He would prefer to ignore the decisive turn of my twenty-seven years, overlooking the question he once posed to himself, or the answer he hides like a shameful address in his wallet. I don't know the answer with any certainty either, but thinking there is an answer already justifies my coming back home and my aspirations.

My father welcomed us with open arms, with that joy he prefers to swallow, which stiffens his back and makes him say, Fine, you arrived in good shape, how is your mother? The years have not been kind to him, as people say when they feel their own age in the gathering wrinkles they see in front of them. My father looks older, but even shorter than I am. His blue eyes are the same as Marcelo's and mine: they remind me of the photographs of me wearing my first suit with long pants, the one handed down from Marcelo years after he was photographed in the same pose. The height, the eyes and the pants give the three of us a family resemblance.

I know he's quite happy, although, really, I don't follow his activities that closely. I can't see him in detail or in perspective; I feel him carefully guarding his isolation. He's very much there, but reserved, like the neighbor we call on who asks us, What can I do for you?—without opening his door. The children will get on his nerves later, but now they amaze and flatter him. Flatter him? I'm using that word without caring if it's the most precise. It seems to fit somehow, because he probably thinks they continue the line but don't best him. They're on their way to where he's arrived, and just like him they'll have to wait a long time before they know they didn't arrive anywhere: that is, to achieve a modest displeasure and enough discretion not to despair and avoid unduly upsetting other people.

I don't know or ask if we're causing any inconvenience. I'm unaware if there's another apartment where he can get away from it all (I'm sure there is); another woman or other people I've never met who can take the place of my mother and us and who will never trust us an inch, hidden decently in a dining room or a kitchen or a bedroom, watching in silence. We're no family. Neither they nor we. Rather, we are families known for their lack of kinship. My brother and I were never born. As children we walked down dead-end streets, to schools with big patios and glassed-in galleries, chilly classrooms and portable altars. As we grew up we had long hair, we began to photograph the world, and followed our mother, isolated, distant, sitting pensively behind her typewriter.

The old folks fall apart; I mean, they slowly begin to separate, without it being too noticeable. They smile, converse, though not much; they suddenly draw a blank on what's being said. They eat at the same table; sometimes they're seen together on the streets. People observing them think they are living in a placid period of final waiting. But no. If one looks closely one will note that they each go down a separate road, drifting apart. They no longer sleep together. If we question them, the reasons they give us are vague. That one can't get to sleep and the other has rheumatism, that they wake up and pester each other, that one wants to sleep on the second floor and stairways are painful to the other. Smoke rings. First there were two beds, now there are two bedrooms, soon two houses. The marriage begins to look like a limited partnership. The partners know each other so well. They communicate by means of gestures. Not even gestures. They look or they don't look at each other and they've already said it all.

When did these folks first sleep in different beds? When in separate rooms? Neither Marcelo nor I could say. One day they were together, the next separate. Affectionate in the manner of casual friends on a trip. Suddenly, a sharp voice, a cutting phrase, a violent gesture that stops midway. They can't tolerate each other. In love, they despise or pity one another. A holding pattern begins. And then what will happen? Domestic tragedy, threats, last words? No. Neither of them has the character for that. They are withdrawn, ferocious and nearly implacable, but timid. They don't forgive anything. They might not reproach or curse each other. But, they don't forget. The insults keep bouncing around inside. But why did they get together in the first place. What attracted them? It seems impossible. It was always difficult for us to imagine that at some distant time our parents were sweethearts. Mother is larger than Father. Reach and weight. In total volume. She is tall and stiff and rather stacked. As her neck is a bit short, her head looks small and round. Her blue eyes glance with a kind of wounded confidence; they would like to smile but become hard and end up observing with distance and severity. She wears gray. Tailored suits. She has a bit of the nurse or the Lutheran lady down-at-the-heels. A daughter of Germans from the south of Chile. Blond tresses, log cabins, immaculate cleanliness, Teutonic discipline. It's somewhat eccentric to be so passionate, sentimental and romantic in a country of crazy Andalusians, not to say gypsies and Araucanians. She had a religious crisis when we started high school. She began reading her Bible out loud and drawing her own morals, which she would then pass on as ultimate truths to her maid. My father closed the door. Classified as a Protestant, she should preach and sing in other houses or in the street. By way of contrast, the old man returned to Mass, took communion, prayed as one possessed in the month of December. It was obvious to my brother and me that we weren't dealing here with a religious war but with something very personal, private. Divorces are not made of biblical interpretations. I imagine my mother was rebelling. I don't know exactly against what. Anything was possible. At night she read Selma Lagerlöf, whom I always thought of as a great armoire with a mirror open on snowy plains. The duel between the two of them must have taken place in the bedroom, behind closed doors. She agitated, her face congested, her eyes flashing, without saying a word. He speaking rapidly to himself. She arranging papers, putting away her typewriter, keeping office hours. He, sarcastic, incredulous, impatient.

    We were already in college when Marcelo told me one day that we were going abroad with her. No one spoke of separation. A "field trip." That's it. These boys need another environment, she said. My father remained silent. Neither for nor against. There was a moment when he seemed offended. "Your mother," he murmured, "has recipes for living, as if life were an apple pie." He sounded resentful. Though she was strict, he too could get his way. Mother followed a certain order, perhaps naive; Father ruled by force, without reasons.

    The three of us emigrated to the State of Virginia. We were incredulous, apprehensive. My mother had the air of a pioneer. The old man stayed tight-assed. He gave us a short farewell hug. I think his hands were trembling.

    Afterwards (in fact there is no clearly defined afterwards), my father stopped being either a hero or a villain and disappeared on a crowded stage. We went away feeling sure one day comes after another, that one night and another night together form a single thread. The abrupt change in languages disoriented us, the colleges had no records or systems, the apartments were smaller and the kitchens were harder to work in. We began to fade away, first our faces, then the lines in our palms; but there were things which distinguished us from each other and yet they too vanished, and I think my mother began to get us confused. Marcelo and I have the same beards; our hair unites us. Marcelo says it reveals my innocence. I say the same of him, but our smiles contradict us.

I returned to Chile for three reasons: my young wife; second, madness is contagious; third, suicide is also very contagious.

But children are another matter. They have heard the noises adults make and they know how we throw ourselves onto the floor, how we bite each other's legs and how we sing off-key in bed. Then, when we decide to tear ourselves to bits in the streets and there are gun butts whacking faces and boots trouncing the belly of the young professor buried alive and hands lopped off a great guitarist, we go out and ask the young people if they still adhere to the Christian doctrine and the Commandments; we accuse them of their lack of charity and respect for institutions, and they respond with sexual wisdom by closing the door on our fingers.

Later, in October, I would see a group of exiles trying to leave. The plane was full of children. The flight for some unexplained reason couldn't take off. The plane spent the night on the runway and the exiles and their children began to stink and get thirsty and approve suicide resolutions.

A boy began to sing and his parents tried to quiet him. But he went ahead and raised his voice, and his song was revolutionary; it insulted the Armed Forces. When he came to the part where the poor would eat bread and the rich would eat shit, after going through several "sons-of-bitches," the soldiers arrested him and his parents, put them in a jeep and, without magic, made them disappear.

Neither his father or his mother scolded him because the child had finally learned his lesson and was showing that you sing when it's hopeless, and the song is accompanied by blows, by blood and unconsciousness, if you have to sing among brothers.

But then, in July, back home for the first time in years, with no chance to write, I thought about what my father calls roots. In reality I was reaching for branches: I would go in and out of stores, stare at the movie ads and newsstands, sit on park benches, get off and on buses, surprised by a city I didn't know anymore, which I couldn't begin to measure in hours or years. Santiago, crowned with snow, was living from shock to shock. Small armed groups would hold up markets, shoot at soldiers or *Carabineros*, blow up gas mains at night and high voltage towers, telephone installations. The truckers had been on strike for months. Food was disappearing. In front of the markets the lines never moved. From the outskirts people walked downtown and walked back home. The city traced and retraced its steps, divided by implacable hatred. Demonstrations and counter-demonstrations. Schoolchildren barricaded themselves behind their desks, workers locked and chained themselves in the factories, businessmen hid in automobiles to sell rotten meat they carted up from the South in suitcases.

The city was like a wheel that begins to stop in a vacuum, losing speed, turning ever more slowly, impelled by invisible gears, and though we know it will stop, it turns one more time, and then again, until movement becomes imperceptible.

During the winter it wasn't as noticeable. People abandon the streets and the squares, they lock themselves up and stare out through the windows of the tall office buildings, pressing their faces to the steamed glass, and they let time pass knowing that something is about to happen—but not yet, wait for the coup. Perhaps it won't even be a coup but a small and precise push to make this gray, icy, humid winter pass and September burst forth in light and buds and flush the mountains with pink again. Suddenly Santiago becomes a vast mall where faceless people move about, a theatre setting whose doors and windows are half open, but as no one enters or exits we cannot tell whether the action has ended or is about to begin.

The lines stretch out, tired, silent. A block of indifferent men and women trying to reach the newsstand where cigarettes are sold, a thick line, disordered, more like a throng that turns one corner and then another, as if the ends tried to meet and swallow each other. Old men and women bundled up, steaming, complaining, inquiring without protesting, imagining, because they can't see them, the steel doors of the Pension Fund, and knowing they will never reach them because there will always be a clerk closing them with chains, repeating: not this month, not yet, the government and the cost of living and inflation, and the planning of Minister Vuscovic plus the U.S. embargo, not to mention the foreign debt and the Paris Club, not this month, they are preparing new forms and there is going to be a bonus, but you forgot the stamps, don't you see, not at this counter ladies and gentlemen, it's not in this building either, can't you understand? Go to the Treasury building, take all your papers, ask for your payment authorization, for your tax receipts, your tax roll number, the permit and the decree, and then ask in the cashier's office, but don't pay until they give you a number, and it's not my fault that people crowd and push, in this country no one dies of hunger, you voted for the Popular Unity so you'll have to put up with it, and don't hold onto the railings because the policeman will smash your fingers, and I am telling you again the doors are already closed, so you'll have to come back tomorrow, what stupid people, why don't you complain to the Comrade President?

But the line continues to stretch, swelling, curling, and now it's not a line, it's an assembly of women who clamor and push and crash against a metallic curtain, and they raise their empty baskets and shopping bags and they'd like to beat someone up, there is no flour or oil or bread, that's a lie, I'm telling you, I've been standing in line all night long and I know, even if you do tell me I won't believe you, because they were unloading last night and this morning early, that might be so but I don't see why you say it, there's nothing inside, the grocer is hiding, yesterday he fired into the air, he has a fortune hidden. The line loses shape, the women wrapped in their shawls push too much, this is not politics, you call starving kids politics? There's no milk or sugar, call the cops, someone should come and open that damned hoarder's door. And then the line will form again into a double line, coiling, without pushing, and in minutes it will curl around the corner, but minus bags and baskets, it's gas containers now and I'm telling you we've run out, there isn't going to be any so don't send your children because all they do is bother me, who said tomorrow? The company is in Monjitas, not here, take the shady side of the street, and I'm telling you not to bug me DON'T BUG ME, they'll knock the fence down, officer, shit what stupid people, there isn't any, can't you understand? The line continues to grow, a thick boa, hissing, slowly unfolding, dense, cold, nauseating, toward one hospital and then another, and then in front of the Emergency Entrance, it crosses bridges and strangles trains and buses, a line of coal and cement, of copper and oil, a thick snake, green, black, silver, red, winding through the market and the shops, from one side of the city to the other, through docks and offices, warehouses and storerooms, a line of empty ships, a line of asphalt and stone. Chile is one huge line. Hey, look at it on the map, a blue and white and brown line. It has always been a line, but not like the one that strangles us now, this dirty, bedraggled muffler that hangs from the neck to the ground and gets caught in the legs. There is nothing. Tell me what's left. Santiago. The buildings downtown are closed, the shops are only half-open, the banks and the insurance companies rusting, the jails open even on Sundays, the butcher shops are full of hooks stained with dry blood, and on the counters stacks of bones. But people don't die, they wait, neither advancing nor retreating, reading alarming headlines in the newspapers.

Down Providencia comes a long line of women shouting and beating pots and pans, down Teatinos Street groups of teenagers, in sweaters, their faces covered with handkerchiefs, wearing helmets and carrying sticks and chains, march at a quick pace, compact, dragging their feet, marking time:

Allende, son of a bitch,
He's going to fall in a ditch . . .

On the road to San Antonio striking truckers hide in the bushes counting their buckshot and setting their nail traps; commandos who will blow up the pipelines and the high voltage towers take position and aim; a freedom march arrives from Arica screaming; another line of trucks searches for its final resting place in the hills over Valparaiso; in the bay, under cover of fog, a gringo fleet levels its guns; on the docks a wet and faded sign says *The PU is screwed, be safe with UNITAS;* acrobatic pilots appear in the sky drawing a white line, but that white line started in Panama, sir, and goes all the way down to Magallanes; the planes write Djakarta in the sky and the letters last only a moment and then dissipate in the mountain gusts.

Finally all the lines are laminated together to form one huge tail that wriggles through cities and ports, parks and deserts, like a living labyrinth without beginning or end. Chileans wait for the coup to be done with, so they can enjoy spring again, and the coup is an empty truck that comes from the South and comes from the North, halting, grinding uphill, until it almost stalls, and finally stops at dawn, douses its headlights and draws out its small shining muzzles.

Seeing the shops shut, the downtown deserted, the small markets and corner stores at half mast and selling under the counter, listening to the easy-going relatives complaining too, desperate now because there is truly nothing available, while lucky people from uptown travel by car to the scene of the crime and pull into a circle around the taxi drivers and truckers who distribute meat, oil and enough whiskey to bathe in, at the blackest price in the history of Chile, it was obvious the circle was about to close.

One would mull over strange ideas, though one more than others: If the country is falling apart, is routed, why the inactivity of the Popular Unity government? No one works, or almost no one, neither the coupon clippers who walk through the streets with a smile a mile wide, nor the government employees, the doctors, lawyers or store managers. They stay home reading the newspapers or keeping a close watch on their TVs. The Workers' Federation says NO to civil war. The workers take over the factories, the industrial belts are tightening with a secret knot that frightens the pot-beating women. Why doesn't Allende defend himself? Why doesn't he take the offensive? The coup is coming? The coup is coming. What can we do?

During a family gathering I witnessed a curious debate among young people who felt responsible for the coming debacle; and each one, in his own sense of defeat, offered a way out which, in my opinion, leads to the same abyss. The young girl who works in a beauty parlor says: Power to the people, attack, strike before they do! You ask me how, what do you mean how, with the industrial belts, of course. But the dentist answers: We are not ready for a confrontation, it would be a massacre. Read *El Siglo,* comrade. The beautician argues that the people are armed. The student of architecture timidly refers to the "comrade soldiers and the comrade *Carabineros.*" Dentist: You've seen what happened to the sailors who conspired with Altamirano—they were jailed and tortured. Read *Punto Final,* then. You spend your time reading and don't know what's going on in the streets. I'm talking about the skirmish between the workers of SUMAR and an Air Force contingent. They fought with small arms; the factory whistles blew and units from the industrial belts and the squatter settlements appeared. The Air Force men retreated. A victory for the people? Nobody took it that way. It was an exploratory mission by the Air Force to test the enemy, to gauge the degree of resistance and analyze the unknown factors. How do the soldiers of 1973 react to the working class? That's what I'm talking about, the comrade draftees. The comrade what? Let me finish. The draftee who hails from the countryside, the barrios and the outlying provinces, who's been listening for some time to the workers, the students and the activists defending Allende, and for whom certain words like "expropriation," "nationalization," "intervention" and "inflation" mean a lot, who has seen the marches and listened to thousands shout *Allende, Allende, the people all defend you!*, who knows there are lines for everything and food baskets for the poor: what does he say, how will he react? I'm not the only one who speaks of the people's resistance, that nightly shuffle of sandals through the shantytowns and that clink of weapons appearing and disappearing. What do the soldiers think of the middle-level purges? And of the generals who are falling by the wayside? What will the soldiers do at the moment of truth? Look, the Air Force took their puppies down to SUMAR to pinion the workers. They retreated, but I don't think there was any sudden panic among the officers. My question, then, is how long can the workers resist? The dentist steadies his glasses. Has anyone asked himself if this general rehearsal is an exact indication of the proportions of the confrontation? I think that Allende realized months ago the shape the conflict will take; it won't be between the forces of the extreme Right and the extreme Left, with the armed forces divided in the middle. No, things are much more serious. We've lost our chance. To arm the people these days is to send them to a collective suicide. And what do you suggest? I'm not suggesting anything, but we can discuss the reasons for the indecision, especially after the rally in June when political conscience reached a height of radicalization and the slogan *Power to the People* was strong. Allende, with 600,000 people marching the 4th of September and swearing to defend him, knows what he's doing, but it's possible that his policy is also suicidal. I'm judging it according to what he has stood for, what he has managed to do and what he has not done. The beautician tells him: Comrade, let's discuss the second element behind the growing sabotage against the popular government. I'm willing to accept that we are living in a strange sort of nightmare, in which we are both victims and accomplices: victims because the coup will be against us and I doubt we can defend ourselves; accomplices because we want to run and yet we don't run, and we want to shout and our tongue is tied, so we let the whole structure collapse on top of us and the monster strangle us. Just like in nightmares.

Supreme architect: Let's suppose a partisan observer had directed and programmed the events that were to occur between 1972 and 1973 so that Allende could be overthrown. Let us suppose that such an observer could have had alternatives, say: on the one hand a plan for a violent attack, a super-abundance of military power to produce a mortal coup, a *coup de grâce*, and on the other hand, the possibility of a gradual weakening, an economic offensive, key strikes, hoarding and black marketeering, sabotage, the complete saturation of the national psychology with panic and discouragement, an old-fashioned coup, a relatively peaceful transition back to the old order of things. Common sense tells us that the second option would have been chosen. But, in these things the sense which dominates is not exactly common: someone decides to adopt the second plan, which is carried out to the next to the last act, and then, at the decisive moment, it's abandoned and the plotters fling themselves back into the first plan of attack.

While I listen to these speakers I think of the hardships they bear. Although they eat, they have to spend, naturally, more than usual, more each time. The black market gets dirtier and dirtier. The newspapers read by the dentist and the beautician and the architect and his wife inform them that the international credit agencies have clammed up for Allende, while they ply the Armed Forces with a glut of sweets, that Anaconda has started a pirate war against Chilean copper shipments, that the government would never be able to obtain spare parts for the truckers because the U.S. refuses to send them. Other speakers, from Ahumada Street and Huerfanos Street, for example, comment on hoarders' cellars, sealed and secret as bank vaults, on the superfreezers that look like frozen zoos, on the supersonic flight of dollars and the delicate pirouettes and falls of the shrinking and expanding Chilean currency.

El Mercurio released its editorials like heavy bales:

Allende has led the country to chaos and to the edge of civil war. Chile? Full of foreign extremists who plot a Cuba-style dictatorship. The country is sinking, we must save it. Allende must resign. Let the military come. Or, better yet, let the military come and Allende leave.

Meanwhile the Fatherland and Liberty Movement doesn't need any speakers: its members are planting bombs, even in the cemetery. 250 incidents in one month. Radio and TV towers fall, water mains explode. When there is no one left to shoot they begin to shoot each other. One of their leaders, nicknamed Houdini, appears-disappears-appears in an airplane between San Carlos, the sea and Mendoza. He comes and goes, skimming the roof of the central police station, landing on top of the Supreme Court and taking off again.

It's been raining but now it's clearing. I'm going out to look for roots. They're in a low gray sky, close by the benches of Plaza Brasil, wrapped in thin blue smoke, moist, woven into dry fig trees and knotty cherries, abandoned patios, tin roofs and brick-and-lime walls, sticking the red plaque of the Heart of Jesus to the dull streetlights that have suddenly lent me a yellowish pallor among the men and women dressed in mourning who pass by in slow motion. The smell of wet wood joins me momentarily to this bench: it must've been summer then and boys and girls spinning through the plaza like figures on a silent carrousel, the slight perspiration of my girl friend soothes me. I let myself go in a long, dizzy embrace; the hooting of a factory siren comes from so far away; a circular ballet of miniature couples, silent, entwined in childhood kisses; my girl friend is wearing gloves because her skin is irritated by an infection; I love you, my darling, she says; the words are incongruous because she stole them from a bolero; old men leave the movie theaters shuffling their feet; the sky smells of dry grass and mint, but on her it looks like honey, and I fondly remember her green skirt, her white blouse; I kiss her neck and I touch her gloves and breasts; and now the plaza shimmers again in semi-darkness, cars go by splashing water and mud; I breathe deeply the rain, the sky, a bit of smoke along the ground. It's my open city.

I get on my motorcycle and go up San Diego Street, Avenida Matta, Gran Avenida, studying everything—the half-opened windows, marked doors, signs of something or someone I've been looking for—feeling the union of the night, the streets and the loneliness, in some man or woman who refused to touch me, who didn't let me get close, but whose smell I still carry in my body, and I would like to conquer our emptiness, the root that keeps us crying together, but there are only corners and blocks, missing relatives, unnamed and unnumbered bus stops, the nearby breathing of those of us falling in the city before we reach our terminal.

I come to wage war.	*Angel González, who*
To wage war on the fields	*wrote these lines, has*
of Castille.	*looked on me from a dis-*
Tired	*tance, his white beard and*
of mounting.	*wild hair, and in his eyes*
Horse, my	*I saw a weariness that has*
horse: rest a while.	*not yet begun; but there*
Now is the time to	*he is, bloody and breath-*
make love under the	*less, like this wound in*
linden trees	*me today; I come from*
lit up by March.	*waging a war, but I've*
(I go away dreaming.	*run out of time.*
I come from a dream.)	

Afterwards I examine two snapshots of Luz María: In one she is running through the rooms of our house in Virginia and the boys are right behind her: they are running away from me because she told them I was about to stab them. In the other she stands on a shaky balcony on the seventeenth floor about to jump, wearing only a green transparent nightgown, her arms outstretched, the sky full of clouds, and down below heavy oaks; the night and the cries of birds have passed. In one snapshot I stand by Luz María, and it's true I deliberately began to fade out of the picture.

Luz María was the girl friend I never talked to: I made her up out of familiar things I saw at dusk in Forestal Park and Plaza Ñuñoa, things which I put together at night lying next to an open window, breathing silently like the trees, dreaming, sliding her across my chest, until I couldn't stand it any longer and I slid her across my belly with the palm of my hand, a whirling palm tree wet with fresh-smelling dew, an explosion of light on a red blinking stem, alive, on fire, and soon faint. Standing like a warrior on the corner of Purísima Street, a few steps from her door, I would whisper to my brother, waiting for the apparition which never appeared. It was enough to know she was inside, sensing or suspecting our nightly visits. What did she do in that house? I will never know. I was in love with myself and it hurt. But during the Month of Mary I would go to Viñita Church to catch her scent along with the lemon blossoms and the candle smoke, praying with the choir insistently, stumbling along, almost screaming with satisfaction near the end because our knees would hurt so much.

I never discussed my religious faith with anyone, especially the nocturnal crises from which I always returned wet and repentant. Or the guilt, because it wasn't rational. My whole life moved like a thermometer: from the chest to the belly to the underbelly. I wrote a poem entitled "The Fountain of Youth" to explain why the member always goes to the sacrifice, while the other two things swing outside and must be bells; the one is a cyclops and the others are blind men's guides. It didn't sound convincing so I tore it up. Instead I remember writing a notebook full of love poems in the style of Becquer and giving it to Luz María, who received it nervously, stuffed it in her school bag and never mentioned it again.

I've said religion was never discussed. It blended, I see now, with a tendency to efface myself; that is, to think of myself as a cosmic being, an adolescent who could fit into any shape or person, who should be received without question, accepted and loved for himself, made up of incomplete but active traits, not altogether under control. I was conscious of my head but not of the rest of my body (my cock was independent); I noticed that my nose grew suddenly when a girl told me so. The arguments about the existence of God which Father Ladrón de Guevara sent up like smoke rings into the air with his deep voice, resonant and bland, didn't touch me. St. Thomas' proof and his metaphor of first causes would get mixed up with the image of the clock and its creator, to which several listeners in the classroom would object that, even if God were everywhere, he was not and did not want to be a maker of clocks or watches.

That the world had a beginning is not important to me. In fact, it annoys me. As far as God is concerned, the world shouldn't have a beginning. In the afternoon classes Father Alvarez repeated the proofs of God's existence, but then my stomach would growl and my throat would fill up with saliva. I didn't listen to Alvarez, tall and skinny, strangled by an enormous Adam's apple, hiding his vast hands like oars under his black robe, then taking them out to make gestures. The Dominican habit seduced me at a tender age and I told everyone my desire to enter the priesthood. No one paid any attention. I wanted to suffer, for people to say: There goes brother Cristián; he sleeps under the stairs, reeking in rags like Saint Alexis, wearing the remains of Housse Partie around his neck. Or to be stupid and sweet like Francesco, or a martial preacher like Father Melero, who after he was a captain in the artillery became a priest in Recoleta. I was never attracted to Saint Augustine or any of the other brilliant sinners—they scared me; not even to the Christians in the arena—I could never quite tell them from the lions. Nero attracted me because I was afraid of him; I found him wise and elegant. I was terrified of my parents' friends and relatives, whose self-confidence I considered a symptom of cynicism. Their houses set my teeth on edge; so did their conversations and their children, their taunts, their insolent and obscene laughter. My saints were long-suffering, complex, gentle suicides, who climbed on the cross shaking their heads baffled by the ferocity of their fellow men. I made my teachers nervous. My parents never said anything around me. I awakened sympathy in women and also wished to awaken it in men, who said I was too intelligent. To some I was a boy-man. To most, a wise monkey.

If faith was not a routine, nor understood, and if it was inconsistent but strong, where did it originate? Possibly in the indifference or ignorance of my father, or in the domestic way my mother managed to be completely wrong—thinking (my God!) her natural sanctity preserved her from the pitfalls of the world and the depths of hell. Such tricks of the devil only left me with the whiff of brimstone, not its taste or fire or the dream of redemption. To me faith meant sinning, since sinning was the only thing that gave any meaning to my prayers, confessions and communions. I didn't understand it that way, naturally, but that's the way I lived my faith, from church to church, from altar to altar, searching for cool, mysterious shadows, soft noises, rosaries, chords, solitudes, direct dialogue with the images and the paintings, defiant acts—praying in the streets, kneeling suddenly in the park, believing in the flight of the Image of the Virgin and in the miraculous pieces of Fray Andrecito's habit, knowing I was predestined. I was never sacrilegious or blasphemous. I always sinned through sex and repented and was forgiven. From the very beginning I kept up direct, secret communication with the Virgin and Jesus. My religion was and is the Mother and Son.

I have to insist on these things and make them clear, because they essentially explain my disagreement with the Father.

I really don't know why the Mother separated from the Father.

On the morning of the 11th of September I awoke with a start. In that first brief moment I didn't know if it was the presence of someone or a noise. I thought of the door. I had put the chain on, and the latch bolted both locks. The noise wasn't coming from the hall or the kitchen, it was coming from the whole floor. Lying on my back, leaning up on my elbows, I stared at the shutters. The apartment was rocking like a glass cage. In the half light I saw the lamp was also moving. I got up. My father was still asleep with his door closed. I turned on all the lights and walked unsteadily down the hall to the living room. The roaring noise stopped. But I heard noises outside and steps on the terrace upstairs. I lit a cigarette and stared out at the shadows running down Alameda. I noticed some movements on the roof of the house next door. I went back to the bedroom and turned off the light, closed the door and stood next to the window, feeling guilty, looking out that way from our 12th floor, unseen by anyone. But the figure on that roof fascinated me. Someone, a young man, was smoothly, delicately, sliding open a slab on the roof. He stuck his head through the hole, then without looking backwards, without even thinking that someone like me might be spying on him, he stretched out his right arm and started firing, in a sort of absurd way because he had a small-bore revolver in his hand that went off without even an echo, just a sharp report, like a firecracker, lost in the city dawn. I could see his dark hair and his striped shirt. He fired for a while towards the Alameda and then, with the same care and precision, he climbed into his hole, moved the slab and closed the roof. I didn't see his face, neither that morning nor the following night, nor all the other nights when he fired from there until they killed him.

I went back to the living room and picked up the phone. It wasn't even six yet. I had a mission to fulfill, and with my camera I would have to go to Tomás Moro, Allende's house. Marcelo was supposed to pick me up at eight. Although I had to call Luz María, I didn't exactly know what I was going to say. I could talk about the tremor or the planes, about the small helicopter that buzzed over the roofs of the San Borja Towers, where my father's apartment was, or I could confess that knowing the danger and feeling trapped I had changed my plans and was going to ask Father Juan to put me up at the monastery. I dialed Luz María's number, let it ring twice, hung up and dialed again.

"I was just thinking about you," she said.

"And the children?" I asked.

"They're still asleep."

"Did you see the planes?"

"They were skimming over the roofs. Then they came back in a few minutes."

"Now that we can go back to sleep the lions in the zoo are raising hell," I told her. "They must be scared."

I thought to myself they should throw the lioness in with them and imagined them jumping around gnawing each other among the eucalyptus, rolling in the gutter and coming out all muddy, dragging the lioness by the nape, like cats, and writhing till they passed out on the horse and donkey carcasses all over the floor.

I continued: "The sun is coming up in the park; I can see light through the blinds. The dogs are making a racket down there too. And a guy in the house next door began shooting."

"Who is shooting?"

"I don't know, someone down there. Nearby."

"And the dogs?"

"You know the ones, the woolly bitch looks like a schoolgirl lying on the grass, gazing towards the river, maybe she hears the lions too. There are about seven dogs from the slums of Bellavista, dripping wet, with their tongues hanging out. The horny bastards. I can't tell if that's foam coming out of their mouths, I hope it's steam, I can't see that far.

"Do you want me to come over?" she asked.

"Not now. I'll call you in a little while. I want to talk to Marcelo."

Later, drinking black coffee, I thought, looking through the twisted slats of the Venetian blind, I might have invented the park, but not the noises or the lions and dogs. Luz María wouldn't hesitate to come, leave the children, take a bus. She would be tangled up over and over again in this sheet I use to cover and uncover her with each time as if it were the first time. Luz María, a small white statue with soft down and tanned belly, a bun on the nape of her neck and a sad mouth, and I, easing my beard between her round breasts, searching for some meaning in her long legs, breathing in the smoke of felled trees and the cool mist of the southern-most islands she brings from the South, deciphering the way of that routine never completely learned. I know that today, at this hour, facing the dawning park, seeing the smoke that rises from the ferns and the dusty silver acacias, by the yellow paths, close to the river's wall, she will be here, and it will be like the first time.

The phone rang again.

"Do you want to meet me at Baquedano?" Luz María asked.

"Now? It's not even six o'clock yet, and I have to go to Tomás Moro. Well, just five minutes, a cup of coffee."

I dressed and went out hugging the wall, my coat collar turned up and hands in my pockets. Nobody on the streets. I thought that night I would have to speak to my father and give him my gun. Later. A little traffic on the other side of the park, a few taxis, no buses. I was surprised to see just a couple of cops at the American Consulate. I was used to the huge green cages, the plastic shields, the riot squad trucks filling with water. Plaza Baquedano was deserted. I looked out at it from my corner, next to Bustamante Street. The old lady in the newspaper stand poked her nose in her cup of coffee. Luz María didn't take off her raincoat. She lit a cigarette. I kissed her hands. There was another couple close to us, the woman doubled up over the table, the man whispering in her ear. When Luz María began to drink her espresso I saw her hands were trembling: "Last night, after supper, the same old argument began. I stated my position. They told me it was like listening to a cassette of *El Siglo*. My poor mama sounds like an old fossil but she chokes on the words."

"What are you going to do with the children?" I asked.

"They'll stay with her."

"I'll have to go away, if only for a few days. Besides, the old man won't want to move."

"What happened?" she asked.

"I don't exactly know what happened."

Luz María looked at the clock, said something else

about the children, something I don't remember, and I kept thinking what it would be like if we could live as the rest of the world, without having to explain anything. But Luz María was tying the belt of her raincoat and I was pleased that she looked distant again, worried about something besides me, willing to help me but also ready to leave.

Later on that morning of the 11th, I went to La Moneda in Allende's famous blue Fiat. A unique mission: to photograph certain details of something that, once consummated, would reach epic proportions. The country is being saved. NO TO CIVIL WAR. How? Who can save the country from an armed struggle? These questions don't work out. Things don't follow anymore. Politics is a game of cards. Cut and shuffled daily. The card game of professional politicians. Outside, in the streets, another game is taking shape. And it has nothing to do with cards. It's possible that the people—disdained and forgotten when they don't try to march—will say suddenly: YES TO CIVIL WAR. Because they feel in front of them a road that opens abruptly. No one thinks of alternatives, then, or consequences. But, where are the arms? This battle which begins in familiar surroundings and extremely loudly will not be maneuvered from outside.

Allende rides with his chauffeur, his bodyguards and his political advisor. They speak as if in asides, without really feeling the words. Keeping my mouth shut, I move my camera, aiming and shooting. I think of Marcelo who would like to be in my place, and of Luz María. If she saw me, she might come to admire me.

The President was saying to his political advisor: "I could write it tonight or, better yet, dictate. I could give you the gist right now."

He becomes thoughtful, though something may have caught his eye on the last corner we passed. The street is empty. Traffic will start up on Providencia. It's possible, perfectly possible they will try something. One or two trucks would be enough. Put the second one at that tight curve on

Eleodoro Yañez, just before Providencia. That's how I'd do it. But what good would it do now? They've got all the aces.

Allende keeps speaking with the same voice he had yesterday and for the last few months, in that paternal tone he's picked up, wise but tired. It's a counterpoint to the right-wing stridency. He's the man who has nothing to lose . . . 10 million people yell fire, trampling and crushing each other in one narrow doorway, he tells them to be calm. Can't you see that the people, all the people, are with me? Stand in lines, be calm, there is no need to be apprehensive, and please, no empty sacrifices or useless heroic gestures. But he said the other day at Tomás Moro that the alternatives are simple: he will complete the people's mandate, finish his term and go home; or he will die assassinated.

What is he thinking now? He looks out the window and seems serene. Crossed hands, fingers intertwined, freckled skin with red hair. Rigid, a cold stare behind thick glasses. Fearless? Irresponsible? Not at all. He's going to his office to fulfill his duty.

"The final version of the speech," Allende says, "was drafted last night. We will go on the air at twelve or a little after. But not in the afternoon. Make sure we can go on nationwide before two."

"The meeting at the Technical University is off, right?"

"No. We should be able to settle this thing soon enough. If everything's under control by 10 we go to the University."

The advisor tries to say something but is interrupted.

"Yes, comrade, I understand perfectly, but I don't agree. We'll give an alert but let's not stir things up and provoke another crisis."

And the military people purged recently? And the stacked deck held by the generals? What's up? Do you know? Don't you?

He continues to stare at the houses, trees, streets, that disappear as we pass by. I know that Allende knows. I think I understand why he's calm. He looks at the time. It's been ten minutes since we left Tomás Moro. One can't speak now of forebodings. If we know anything it's because the facts are spread out on the table, face up. No intuitions. For me it's the last day; I don't exactly know what will happen. Today, as I write this, I think of him and of myself. Chileans will finally understand what pathetic dreams their myths were made of. Not Allende. He never saw the myths around him, only men and women instead of shadows crowding about him. He has struggled and made sacrifices for them, flaring in anger when he looked underneath a uniform and found nothing, reprimanding the youth who won't talk with him but would waylay him arrogantly with a bomb in hand. Patrician, white-haired, virile, suddenly pugnacious and hot-headed, he is trying to make a revolution. And this with Chileans who don't want a civil war, bur rather a kind of peace that combines considerate oligarchs, long-suffering workers, a middle class that will somehow make ends meet, and the armed forces, whom everyone respects because they can overthrow governments, any government they please. Allende expects to last three more years . . .

We're past the dangerous corner. I don't know which car we are in the formation: the last or the middle? Allende wants the radio. Any station. Music. Another. The same. Put on some news, he says. The driver searches and searches. The funny thing is the music sounds all the same. They are playing marches, and at first I don't recognize them, but soon I do. They are German marches, I tell him. I remember a war movie, says the driver. Why, asks the President, what movie? Haven't you seen it? These are marches from a Nazi film. Another station, comrade, put on the news. But now the stations are falling silent, falling off the dial. Allende notices it. A silence remains that fills with static, and then another sound, distant, near, distant again. A formation of planes flies over us, out of the leaden sky and into the clouds over the sea. Allende looks at them and says nothing. They disappear. They've probably looked on us as a curious group of wheels and blue roofs romping down the Alameda. Maybe they didn't even see us. I think for them we no longer count.

I would like to say goodby to Allende but I realize this would be completely absurd. No one is thinking of goodbys except me.

"Listen," he says, "find Olivares and tell him we are ready to go on the air."

The Fiats stop suddenly. Doors open and close noisily. I can hear the hollow sound of weapons being readied. Near our Fiat is a swarm of bodyguards. I see muzzles and triggers everywhere. The palace guard rigidly comes to attention. Allende gets out, salutes, enters La Moneda rapidly. He has an automatic rifle in his hand. One bodyguard walks on his right, slightly ahead of him, his finger on the trigger, observing everything, moving steadily but gracefully. Something of Kung Fu in his actions, but also a down-to-earth grace, cool and fast, opening, closing, turning, advancing a few steps and imperceptibly retreating.

Stunned, I remain. I would have liked to shake his hand. I wouldn't have known what to say, whether to warn him or cheer him up. The flag blazes over La Moneda. I want to tell him he is a good man, that he doesn't deserve this fate, that he isn't getting out of a '73 Fiat, but really he's stepping out of the 19th century, from the old Republic. It's just a conspiracy, an insurrection, secret agents everywhere, truckers with dollars, cunning and devious enemies who know how to strike and then hide. Nothing more. To say nothing else to him, but to see in his eyes one more time, the last, the sadness of a brave and wounded man, and to let him see the same sadness in mine. Nothing else. But he is already inside and lost in the Winter Garden. I see his back. He's forgotten me.

Later, at home again, the phone began to ring. At first we didn't pick it up. My brother was already home and he answered one call but didn't understand the message. I took the phone and the voice I heard sounded disguised, and I was invaded by a sense of imminent danger. I told him to hurry and tell me what the hell he wanted. He was lying or confused. I hung up. We went out on the terrace to try and see the battle on the other side of the river. A jeep on patrol came down Merced. We heard a scream and a burst of bullets hit the side of our building. In

Plaza Baquedano an infantry detachment was taking up positions. The little green soldiers ran crouching, hugging the ground, then threw themselves on the grass and aimed at the Alameda. They waited without moving. From the terrace, at that distance, they looked like a detachment of disciplined lizards. Machine guns started firing. And at that moment, from behind the Law School, snipers also opened fire. Then, a kind of disorderly dance began. The little soldiers ran between the benches of the square, shooting on their knees, on the ground, with the skill of trained cowboys, and the bullets from the other side of the Mapocho River came ricocheting, echoing from San Cristóbal hill to the Orient Restaurant. Then armored cars and artillery arrived. It was weird seeing that tiny army locked inside the open star of the Plaza Baquedano. The crossfire isolated it in green scenery with the mountains fading in the distance. Someone was running away across Pío Nono Street shooting. The bullets whistled all around us. The neighbors were lying flat on the ground. The terrace had glass all over it. Scared voices rose from below. When there was no more shooting the soldiers returned to Plaza Baquedano, people appeared again and some even went down to the park. A curious battle was fought among families anxious to go out and fly their flags. The forces of order were chasing an invisible enemy. All activities ceased. Neighbors went out to comment on the combat alternatives. From the rooftops behind a building shotgun blasts were booming.

    I picked up the phone and told Father Juan I was on my way. The street seemed peaceful. Except that on leaving our building I was surprised to see a face I knew, beady eyes fixed on me, unblinking. The widow was not staring at me openly. Later she would watch me night after night through the peephole of her apartment, while I stood guard at the entrance of our tower in San Borja.

                      I would like to mention here something that happened a short time afterwards: a conversation about lay brothers which had some personal implications.

Next to the glass door of the second patio of the monastery, Father Juan, wearing civilian clothes, points at me and says something clearly stemming from our surroundings and requiring our awareness of the flowers, the stakes and the trees. You can't quite see them in this early morning light, but sense them making a station that Christ hasn't stopped at yet. Nothing, he says, can halt the movement of this tragedy born like a somber spring. We could help it be more creative, give it depth, sap, strength, but not interrupt it, or even reduce it, in its path of bloodshed. To confuse it with a peace that changed into apathy would be blasphemy. Blindness. Who can say Jesus didn't call on the fighters? To talk of birth is to summon them. If battle terminology scares you or the idea of combat, it is because you identify war with death.

Custodio, the fireman-priest at my side, is wearing his black uniform: a jacket, rubber pants, and knee-high rubber boots. The large frightened eyes are also black, but on his waxen face, not stamped but always changing, is engraved the death of all those people he saw shot a few hours ago. He tells us he's just come from a basement in La Moneda Palace full of water and smoke, where soldiers, moving with great, slow gestures, were shouting commands before machine-gunning. He says he saw members of the palace guard trembling and moaning, and two puddles of blood, one larger than the other, like lights on the floor, where Augusto Olivares, Allende's close friend, fell. He doesn't understand all this talk about youth and springtime, while shots are still bouncing off the walls of ministries, and from San Cristóbal hill you can hear the echo of small arms and the muffled sound of bodies tumbling from tin roofs all morning.

But he is not talking to Father Juan—he's talking to me, and I haven't said a word. I have the feeling he thinks he saw me in that basement and doesn't understand why I'm here, safe. In his gravedigger eyes I see surprise and resentment. Father Juan is like a beautiful stringed instrument in that lush garden. In the background stands the huge palm with that old wound on its throat made by Brother Luís, hatchet in hand, completely insane; rose bushes drowning in a grass nobody bothers to cut. Father Juan speaks, the birds respond, his tongue goes back and forth against the massive white teeth, his tie rises in the air and he seems to dance, while Custodio and I dodge daggers in the morning light. You see the basement, the smoke, the mud, the cannons, the body of the President which the firemen carry out wrapped in a rug on a canvas stretcher; but you only see the vault, you do not see the life rising over it like a crown of a tree, nor the young people who are still fighting while they build, leaf by leaf, that new tree, and they give it their summers and falls, their songs, hearts whittled out with pen-knives, their initials of love, the clouds that make morning and the caresses with which they gently and mysteriously cover up the roots.

I know I'm listening to a song, but I also know that Juan is singing it thinking something else. He is preparing a sermon, a kind of vigorous outcry against death, to be read the first day of school, and I understand Custodio's confusion and also his distrust. Juan knows that all of Chile is enveloped in a cloud of gunpowder; he also knows that it isn't possible to hasten the spring through pious exhortations. Something like a dam has broken over us. Custodio the fireman cannot untangle his hoses and fireplugs while Juan and I announce aloud a beginning, not a burial.

Custodio's distrust of me stems from the fact that he cannot clearly identify me in the massacre process: he might accept me if I introduced myself as a defender of "Fatherland and Liberty" and leave me alone if he thought I were a clandestine Marxist. But he sees me occupying the cell next to the prior's, seriously interested in the sermon against death, wearing the thick gray sweater Juan has lent me, reading Saint John of the Cross at five in the morning, loading vegetables I bought in the market, boiling water in the kettle at dawn and drinking stiff vodkas at night. He doesn't accept me. I see the doubt in his eyes along with a certain growing resentment. Maybe he's afraid of me. I hadn't thought of that. What does he know about me? No one told him where I came from or why I'm here.

Instead of the present events which should be filling my notebook, I'm attracted to the twisted memory of things long past which set the pattern for my reactions today. Past events hurt like the missing limb of the amputee. I've felt the pain of this obstinate flight before, but I know that next time it will have an added, because involuntary, bitterness.

It seems to me that disappearing into the State of Virginia is not the same as disappearing into the city of Santiago. That's clear, but there's more. In Santiago a person like me can fade away, but the family endures. Our roots intertwine with grandparents who grew horizontally while the country was stretching from Arica to Magallanes. That they abandoned their lands or traded them for factories or lost them in epic payrolls is not something which divides us. On the contrary, it helps bring us closer together. Even so, one mustn't forget certain distinctions. Some are the offspring of landowners, others of overseers and the others of peasants or sharecroppers. I think about the Chileans whose colonial ancestors go back more than a hundred years. I can recall a poem by Pablo Neruda dedicated to Joaquín Murieta, where he mentions almost all these family names; I say "almost" because Neruda omitted the names of the wine-growing families, some of which are also hundreds of years old. We live, therefore, in two houses: one is the landowner's, with gardens, galleries, cool rooms with high ceilings, beds as big as whaling boats, lavender sheets, flowered bowls and washstands, fragrant dining rooms, adobe walls, smoky cast-iron kitchens, sepia portraits, glossy issues of *Illustration* and *Pacific Review*, a house which is a memory of childhood, asleep in the steaming breath of horses disappearing in the southern rains; the other, where my brother and I always lived, is the typical suburban apartment for professionals and office workers and, also, for broke patrician families, or the small row houses of Ñuñoa, or the huge old house unremembered among the cement blocks on Portugal Avenue, or the little brick boxes on Santa Rosa. Nothing more than a few roofs and patios from the past. We Montealegres are old landed bourgeoisie, not wine families, we owned trees and farm land. This was many years ago. My brother and I knew only the decadence of the landowners. Lands without a present or a future. Agrarian reform. A past whose meaning is understood but never questioned—original sin—in novels by veterans like Barrios or bizarre ladies like Bombal. My father should have been a lawyer or a doctor or a priest or, as a last resort, a soldier or teacher. In that order. Poor and proud, he wasn't able to be any of those things. But, since he was what is called "sensitive and artistic," he married the daughter of a German, studied medicine and ended up dedicated to music. I imagine he never seriously thought about his destiny. Instead he divided his life into neat portions. He wanted to conquer and hoard up his inner peace, hidden away in the unreality of a stage, but in atavistically following the rules of the family clan, he jealously guarded a conservative tradition. Another portion was us, whom he obviously couldn't or had no desire to understand. For a half-artist who hides in order to create, a family like ours is a hindrance. Chile is full of gentlemen-artists, men of order and sobriety, some architects, others dentists, doctors, engineers, industrialists or businessmen, who retire to a room in the second or third patio to sin with a pen, a brush or a piano. Respectable citizens who could, if they wanted to, frequent the Club de la Unión. The uproar caused by the people's artists, by communism and free love, came after the 1920's with the de Rohkas, the Románs and Guzmáns, the generation of 1938 and other things from across the Mapocho river. Perhaps unconsciously believing that we were complying with the scruples of my father, my brother and I sympathetically followed the path of the 1950 generation, but though they were well-dressed and well-groomed, these writers and artists turned out to be more alienated, stoned and Catholic than the others. My father criticized our long hair, our hanging shirttails and jeans and our discotheque and Copelia-style English: yet he knew the elegance these things implied.

The truth is I grew up in a Catholic environment, full of respect for the concept of country, decent and introverted, smothered with middle class. Religion, I've already said, was a very intimate way of ennobling my eccentric myths of puberty, but it was also a kind of militancy that saved me from the sordid adventures of some of my classmates at school: I'm referring to a certain dandified anarchy that begins in English-speaking schools, branches out through swanky neighborhoods like Las Condes and Vitacura and Lo Curro, reappears with the resort sun of Papudo, Zapallar and Cachagua and explodes, once every hundred years, in some event like Piedras Rojas: countless thousands of well-fed, dope-smoking hippies listening with rapt expressions of beatitude to the mangy guru from SILO.

They smoked cheap hemp; we waited until we could inhale the Colombian gold, a blend of acacia dust and the neighborhood girls' school, that was burning in clandestine but very clean beds in San Cristóbal. They solved a sexual problem by periodically going to well-established barrio brothels, very macho, like their fathers who graduated from laying the domestic servant to fucking the elegant call girls. We took care of our problem with wild assaults on the whore houses, bathing in violet permanganate, making eternal promises we kept from Thursday to Friday, once a month.

This leads me to things which hurt and shame me. But before I tell you about them I will try to describe Luz María. I will begin by saying there never was any strong inclination on her part to fall in love. That, in my judgment, considering what happened later, has some bearing on the shape of her face, the expression of her eyes, her way of speaking and walking. A small memory may clarify the image I have of her, something that happened years ago when there was a kind of ambiguous relationship between us and I tried to break her down. She was standing in line waiting to get into the cafeteria of the UNCTAD, a UN building, and I was watching her from a distance, sitting on one of the railings of the terrace. It fascinated me to see her advancing slowly, taking small steps as in a religious procession, going into the nave to set down her meal. Luz María—I firmly believed—had come down from somewhere else, and in that line of dark people she shone in my direction. I remember an insistent light that erased shapes and turned the square into an oasis of reflections, absorbing the gray sky, the iron sculpture on the fountain, the whiteness of the tiled floor. The small square opened to receive a sun that wasn't there, a kind of ancient sun that was abandoned by other people who once waited with the same concentration and forgetfulness. The light contributed to her way of being, not to me or anyone else, but only to her. I have never had much luck at describing her: I can visualize her eyes, a movement of her mouth, something that crossed her forehead; on the other hand I recognize her obstinate determination. I can move inside her without words, feeling peace or fear, staring at the still light, understanding her loneliness. Sitting in front of her I pretended to read so she could eat in peace. She told me I looked like a fool staring at her, and that as far as the light she was radiating through her navel was concerned—I must have read that in the stories about the Yaqui Indian, book one. She asked me if I had any money. I said no. I can lend you some, she said. What for? Let's go, she said. And we left. She walked ahead of me because her steps were longer than mine. Her pants weren't tight anywhere. You need to gain some weight I thought. Her sweater seemed to grow on her, like another color of skin, under the straight brown hair. Luz María had a red Mini Austin. She gave me the keys. But where are we going, I asked her. To my house, to get my books, I have classes until five. And what am I going to do? What you always do at this time, she said. Nothing. Well then, nothing. We went to her house and then returned to the Catholic University. Pick me up, she said, at five, don't forget. I sat in the car watching the students going in and out. Near the monument to don Crescente Errazuriz two brunettes were standing, not much forehead but good legs. I stuck out my head and offered them a ride. Where are you headed, little sisters, I said. Downtown, they answered.

Dumb bastard, I was thinking of San Cristóbal, of some drive-in, or at least some side street where I could make a move. Because they looked fuckable. We ended up in Forestal Park. They asked me to take them to Providencia and I waited for them in the car. It was getting dark when they returned and we now went directly to the shadowy groups smoking under the trees.

All this is ancient history and I only bring it up here because of my experience with the navel-light and because it is impossible for me to describe her without thinking of these small gestures or reactions that later could grow and make me afraid of her. Also, because I didn't bring the car back that afternoon, and the following morning when I mentioned the marijuana and that I had gotten spaced and run out of gas on Costanera and that someone apparently had opened the trunk and stolen the tools, and when I gave her back the car keys, Luz María didn't say a word. I don't think she even heard me.

I suppose the mute way Luz María always established her distance is an important part of my memories. I think I didn't matter to her or to her group at the university, or to her family—she lived alone with her mother. What was, in reality, "her life?"

The precocious sociologists of today would say that she and I were the products of "pluralist homes." A euphemism that might suggest promiscuity and desertion. Gabriela Mistral, whom my mother admired because she wore her hair like a man and prayed to Mohammed, said that if the Chilean home exists at all it is because the working woman maintains and sustains it, and when it breaks apart it's because the man goes running off and sows his wild oats in the nearest belly, in order to confirm his original sin.

In time the house on Purísima Street disappeared. Sometimes I think it only existed in my imagination. It probably faded away in the yellowish light of the neighborhood streetlamps.

Luz María appeared in my life, as I said, with a sweater hanging from her shoulders, bluejeans, sandals, long hair floating. You might call it a uniform, but uniforms are often deceiving. There is a superficial upper-caste pluralism in Santiago that functions amazingly on several levels—religious, political, commercial, sexual—but which nevertheless discerns with pointed ferocity the different social strata. A poor girl from across the tracks can dance in a discotheque in Providencia, get stoned in Las Condes, dress up, if she's smart, in a Lo Curro boutique, undress in Viña, but she'll always be a *rota*, that is, punctured, broken from birth.

Luz María's house, a bungalow in Ñuñoa, was situated then between two worlds. The city has zones that are like a no-man's-land. From here she could avoid the descending middle class and, via the Catholic University, open the doors of patrician families. I never met her father, and the times when I gently questioned her about him, she asked if I thought she'd been born by spontaneous generation. The truth was he appeared and disappeared like leap year. He was a lawyer or some kind of wheeler-dealer, and he kept or used to keep, I think, two families: Luz María's, without luxury but on a good middle-class footing; the other, I imagine, in an upper-class neighborhood, in the ghostly, decorous atmosphere of a supermarket.

Luz María was without ostentation or camouflage; she followed my monologues in ironic silence, gave no opinion, contrasted facts. The "New Wave" broke over the university, the church, the drive-in, but it was left knocking at the door of the old mansions. The Christian Left came afloat in the classrooms and yards of the Catholic University. Gringo missionaries with funny looks and accents hung around the Casa de la Luna. They aren't exactly nuns, said Luz María of the young girls with rimless glasses and heavy clogs who installed themselves in the shantytowns to "raise consciousness." But they were. They ended up going back home. The Maryknoll nuns would marry the Maryknoll priests. That's okay. They did no one any harm. Luz María admired Abate Pierre. She collected records with agrarian reform messages. Worker priests in shirtsleeves, quiet people, unionists, were leading her and myself to the industrial belts, to militancy.

I heard her talking one time with a history professor, who was defending his apolitical stance as if it were his virginity. "We the Catholics," he parroted, and remained a moment in silence waiting for his halo to light up, "Fulfill our duties of social responsibility, but politics leads to dogmatism, to violence and to class struggle. No. That, all of that, is miles away from Jesus and the Holy Mother Church. Of course, everything may be found in the vineyards of the Lord."

"Wow, honey! Everything, including hypocritical sons of bitches," commented Luz María. "The vineyards of the Lord! Those are the words of the magazine *Ercilla*, where they still say 'Missy Rosita and don Eduardo,' and figure they're very in with the big landowners and their foundations for poor students and milk-in-the-schools programs.

"All those people stink," she said, "because they never leave the enclosure of their after-dinner conversation, in which they still believe that the way to deal with the workers and the peasants is with charity and a hard fist, as though they were children, so that by virtue of their obedience they will go to heaven. Incredible bastards. The other day one of these jerks told me that Chile belongs to the Spanish aristocracy and its descendants. He told me this with his hair greased up in a butch and the face of a poor slob who's just been fumigated."

The first time I picked her up at her house, Luz María's mother asked me what was my second surname. I said it, and I thought about it, and she thought about it. That was her style. She classified me in silence as if she had the list of names of those who will board Noah's Ark and those who will drown. She didn't argue or insult. The kind of screaming old woman who after fixing her false teeth demands the immediate execution of Allende and the Communists belongs to another group. Closer to the Country Club. Luz María's mother wrote down her relatives' names in her calendar. The word "landed" carried more weight with her than the word of the Vatican. If the relatives whom she named with her tight lips painted in the shape of a heart had received her in their salons, she would have felt more "fulfilled" than Princess Grace of Monaco.

But there, crowded in small rooms, surrounded by

sharp, cold furniture called "modern" because it is plastic, presiding under a watercolor by Pacheco Altamirano that seemed painted with violet "Los Perales" wine, she found herself decisively alone. She was a relative of all the last names in Chile that never were hers. When she said that Uncle So-and-so could become interested in me and make a society photographer, Luz María added that this uncle had been deceased a long time and that the only photos which seemed to interest him, since they were found in his mortuary chamber along with other paraphernalia, were of Parisian girls in lace panties or naked.

One night Luz María told me her mother was shocked at knowing she had "sexual habits." She was waiting for me to ask her what those habits were. But I didn't ask her. And she changed the subject. I came to the conclusion that for Luz María I would always be something at her side, like a husband or a couch. Let me elaborate on that last word.

I would recline under her naked body, long, curving, dark, full of sun, under breasts you can't compare to a fruit—I mean, hard crests with nipples like rings or eucalyptus buds—and as I looked up at her, Luz María would lie there, motionless, her mind on something else, inhaling and exhaling as her hair ruffled and twined in the breeze. The day came when she wrapped herself around me like a vine. Tarzana. And she loved me the way you love a tree. I never understood why. Luz María didn't feel sorry for me. That was proof enough that deep down she was fond of me. Down where? The secret would be revealed slowly. She gave up her "habits," dropped out of school, became my wife, gave birth to two children, and went mad.

Now we, the distinguished Dominican alumni, will speak.

"I went to the priests when I was seven," I say.

"I went in when I was seven, too, in 1925," says Custodio. "So here you are, full of pleasantries and intriguing anecdotes. I would like us to be absolutely frank. Give up foolish inhibitions, let's deal with concrete facts."

"How can I talk about facts? What do I know about what happened between the time I was seven and thirteen? Can you remember that far back?" I ask him.

"Sure, from the time I was spoiled rotten in a penniless home, became a punk who jerked off a lot, a petty thief who couldn't stop his own weight, until a couple years in a public school got me ready for college. I never looked back: I had to get ahead, using everything I could, you understand, everything at my disposal."

"You were not a thief and you didn't break the law. Everybody knows that."

"I told you we should speak frankly. Living around hoods and being a hood gives you a smell that sticks to your clothes. The middle class neighborhood lived in the space of a few blocks. My old man was a small businessman, the neighbor a shopkeeper, another a schoolteacher, the one down the street a painter of saints; we lived in little brick houses. Wealthier ones had a tiny parlor, the furniture shrouded with gray slipcovers. The poorer ones lived next to the counter: the baker, the shoemaker, the undertaker, the delivery boy. Our neighborhood establishments were the 9th precinct, the Buin Regiment, churches, Valentine Letelier school, the #4 Girls' School, the insane asylum in Los Olivos, the morgue, a place that sold marble, the Central Market, the General and Catholic cemeteries, and the shooting range.

Almost all us sons and daughters of shabby middle-class life were able to escape. I'm not talking about those who died in accidents, suicides, consumptives, missing persons, I'm talking about those who changed. There were a few priests. Very few. They dropped out on the trip to Rome or soon after. There were, on the other hand, a few celebrities: a boxer, a gunman, a beauty queen, a circus clown, two army colonels, a psychiatrist, a surgeon. The gunman, until recently, still went in and out of jail like going to a spiritual retreat. Our parents? They died. Completely. It seems their stay in this world was preordained for a single performance. Weddings, baptisms, wakes: the same cake, the same flowers, a few arguments and, in the end, some hole in the wall or the ground. A tango, yes Cristián, a drab little tango. What I'm getting at, though, is not the frame around all these photographs of the dead but rather certain executioners in particular. These are the ones with guns who have started to do to Chile what was always their primary aim: to destroy it."

"No, they haven't taken up arms, it's not them." I say.

"Yes them. Our middle class is indecisive, but if it sees the building about to collapse, it will give it the final shove. The treasury might be empty, but never so empty that it can't come up with another pension. We look up to the winner with envy as we sharpen our claws for his downfall. Maybe you're right. They don't shoot. They only load the weapons of those who do the shooting, if they see victory in the sights. In any case, our sober middle class observes the massacre from too far away, and there are those who get a perverse enjoyment from it, the same as when they see a pig slaughtered or the wringing of a chicken's neck or a rabbit skinned or hot peppers stuffed into a cow. I remember there was a tenement in my neighborhood where a fat old hag lived with a young girl in one room. The old bitch would come home drunk and beat up the girl with belts, sticks and ropes; the girl would howl, the old lady quietly beating the shit out of her, kicking her while she was down, and meanwhile the neighborhood would wait in silence, enjoying in a dirty way the fact that a human being can be kicked, left unconscious, and yet the world does not come to an end.

"Yesterday the police were fishing a corpse out of the Mapocho river. From the truck they took some long poles with hooks on the end. Something like harpoons. I couldn't believe they had special instruments for that type of work. Unless they got them from a circus or a whaling company. On that spring morning, washed with sunlight, under the green willows and the white clouds, the cops were going down among the rocks to the river to remove the deceased-shot-drowned, and up above, on the other shore, a few blondes in gold sweaters and some young men in blue sports shirts, some gentlemen in tweed jackets, and myself, looked down fascinated at the operation. We didn't applaud because no one dared. The only ones who were scared were the girls.

"All this doesn't hurt me but it amazes me. Because I expected the revolution to be made in the name of the great Chilean middle class. In answer to chaos I expected civic order; in answer to the frenzied orgy throughout the country I expected the strong calm hand of decent neighbors, of respected heads of families, wise old men, mature, calm and decided. But the good men locked themselves up in their bathrooms and sat down. My middle class disappeared, literally, it was wiped out like a face in a dirty window in the rain. That big myth, that mattress bearing all blows, accepting punishment with dignity, went to pieces in the air with the straw floating, the stale dust of years living a lie. We hid the body. We kept quiet. A few weeks ago their women were in the streets screaming and pounding on their pots. Tuesday, after the radios announced Allende's imminent fall, the neighbors, our fine poverty-ridden brothers, unfurled Chilean flags and hung them from their balconies. A little later, amid the sound of artillery, airborne rockets, machine guns, of pistols, carbines and revolvers, when the bullets were whistling past our windows and terraces, they went out, crawling on all fours to take down the flags, afraid the *rotos* from the industrial belts would prevail and the hordes would arrive to loot their houses. The history of Chile has been made by the gentlemen and the proletariat. The middle class only writes it down, consolidates it, accommodates it, touches it up and breaks its back, then deposits it in hundreds of volumes which are only good for holding up walls during earthquakes.

"I joined the order in 1925."

When Custodio talks you can hear him like the cannon shot at noon from Santa Lucía hill. Alone, dressed in black, sitting on a rock in the garden, he spits at the sky, stares with his whole face, covers me with his black eyes, sparkling, drops falling from his sleeves and boots. His fingernails are dirty and he smells like smoke.

The afternoon is coming to an end, and now I wouldn't hear him even if he spoke because I'm listening to the palm trees blowing back and forth in the wind. I'm fascinated by the golden thorns and red petals of the quince. A dog barks in the cloister, the sky lightens instead of darkening. I wish I could leave. Get out of here as soon as possible. I keep my jacket ready in my room. But I inhale the blue evening with my whole being; the quivering of the rose bushes is the quivering of the old priests who walk by the cemetery planted with fig and chestnut trees; I can feel in the dry hemlock and weeds a stored warmth I shared with someone I embraced while dragonflies and butterflies flew all around us, hidden in the bushes, our throats dry, exhausted from trying so hard, listening to the distant bells, planning the reconciliation and communion in the sweet hunger of Holy Thursday; the morning, vague and dangerous, noon holy with the scent of old wood and silk ornaments in the sacristy.

"The Christian Democrats were winning the battle," I say.

"For you it was a battle," responds Custodio. "I want to talk about other times, when we were winning—not completely, it's true, but we convinced the authorities and that was what mattered. You are living in a textbook, confusing the issue; you bounce off the edges of anarchism as you discover the Marxist islands in the universities. In a certain misguided but obvious way you try to identify with the people. What does the Falange mean to me? Maritain? It's not as if I closed my ears with disgust or left politics behind. Christianity is the revolution. Juan writes a sermon about spring, or, rather, about childhood; he wants the tree of life to open up for us, golden and fragrant, and swallow the sky and suffocate the fire in La Moneda with its branches; and he wants the birds to start singing everywhere, little birds disguised as hippies, with their long, silky golden hair, and their faces like immaculate buttocks, their white socks, scrubbing the obscenities the Communists scribbled on the walls with a bucket and sponge—all this under the Roman gaze of the handsome, massive mamas of Feminist Power. But I'm telling you that while you are learning Maritain and getting close to Marx and believing in a Catholic Boy Scout named President Frei, we are at another Mass and it has nothing to do with guitars or the Peace Corps: a Mass for the barrio they christened "City of New Havana." Listen:

WOE TO THE RICH!

Come now, you rich, weep and howl for the miseries that are coming upon you. Your riches have rotted and your garments are moth-eaten. Your gold and silver have rusted, and their rust will be evidence against you and will eat your flesh like fire. You have laid up treasure for the last days. Behold, the wages of the laborers who mowed your fields, which you kept back by fraud, cry out; and the cries of the harvesters have reached the ears of the Lord of hosts. You have lived on the earth in luxury and in pleasure; you have fattened your hearts' content in a day of slaughter. You have condemned, you have killed the righteous man; he does not resist you.

JAMES (5:1-6)

"This, little brother, was the gospel read in all the churches in Chile, Sunday, September 16, 1973. What do I care about your clothes, your money, your tapestries, vases, precious ointments, your trucks or truckers? Your Impalas and your tunics, sons of Saks, grandchildren of Tiffany? Little brother, if you want to be a politician, turn to Saint James, let your clothing decompose on your body, fall in love with man and woman, not with pants and panties, talk to God, don't ask Him for an appointment over the phone, search Him out and corner Him, fight it out with Him, smoke Him, run naked and sail with Him, go to jail with Him and get beaten beside Him. Have you smelled Him? He is a smell of both man and woman. Nothing is Him. Everything is Him. When the Christian Democrats were memorizing their catechism, we got the news that God had died. No sir, He did not die. You don't have to be a private eye to find Him, you have to feel and see and touch, the way you put out the flame of a candle. You won't burn yourself; it is simply the point of departure."

Later, without transition, Custodio remarks, "My father opened a small store."

"Well, okay," I say, "on the one hand we have your dry goods store with its wretched smoky rooms, in a neighborhood full of toughs, agreed. The child is ashamed to be middle class, he lives like the poor, his mother has lost her pretensions. If the old man gets rich he goes from the Association of Shopkeepers to the waiting room of the General Manager of the Bank of Chile; and they receive him, not to accept or respect him, but he is tolerated. He goes to Cartagena on vacation and he eats at the Escorial Restaurant. But if the old man goes broke—I understand he did go broke—the pants are patched up, the shirt looks like a sieve, you almost hit the slums, but you save yourself and you put up a last ditch stand in your little row house. What else?"

"He lost what he had for two simple reasons: he was an honest man and he was surrounded by cops. That's it. The store was like a ship's bow, receiving in front the whole run of traffic to the cemetery and all the power turned loose by the August wind and rains. My father erected a huge sign on the roof for Cinzano vermouth; it was a winged horse, blue and red, tied to the tin roof with thick wires. The horse flew. At night, lit up and glistening with rain, it was the only thing alive in that dark, cold street studded with dwarf palms and deep ditches. The riderless horse from his high perch would direct the funeral processions, the black hearses and trains of old Percheron horses, would point the way to the madhouse, the morgue, and finally to the little plaza in front of the cemetery."

The 9th precinct was half a block from the store. The cops would come in to drink big carafes of wine and eat huge sandwiches of spicy sausage. They would then fill their saddlebags with enough food for a month, sign the credit ledger and take off. They never paid. They thought they were doing their duty protecting the old man from hoodlums. But some sergeant had a better idea. He organized some detectives and goons, teamed up with a servant girl who at the right time would drug the whole family, and he'd come in with his partners to steal the entire inventory. They carried the food off in trucks and the money in sacks. Then came the business of fingerprints, photographs and interrogations. Nothing was ever recovered. Another sergeant—maybe the same one—told my father to burn down the store. He would be taken care of. Burn it and get the insurance. It was too late. The old man looked at him morosely.

"From the store, we moved to rented rooms. My father went north. From the boarding house we moved to an abandoned lot with a shack. The ground, muddy and sinking in the August frost, suddenly flowered: it was covered with mushrooms—and from then on we were street vendors. My mother sold coal, one of my brothers became a mechanic on 10th of July Street, and the other was a salesman in a small store on San Diego. They freed themselves. The old man? He must have died. My mother and a kid brother are living in a barrio. Surviving. Barely. They all worked for me.

"Me, a seminarian, a priest, the great Custodio, expert in canon law; I would take them a basket every week and say Mass in the slums. The last one was an outdoor Mass. I don't really know who I said it for. There was no one there. Just tin cans, old buckets, rotten wood in the ditch. I think there were clothes hanging from the light poles. There weren't any animals. No one was left. I remember my father's face when he discovered the theft that ruined him; he must have kept that expression until the day he died and I inherited it. It was waiting for me in the slums Sunday the 16th. The same face."

I would like to continue this dialogue, knowing no one will listen to us. My father decides he's an artist because he's no good at handling money or cow manure or cow udders. The family pushes him to one side. The land doesn't produce much. Just debts. You end up asking for work, or rather a pension. But the Chilean family, like their religion, is one of a kind. No matter how low we stoop we don't stop being our surname, or a cousin, nephew, uncle or grandchild. Whatever. Live in Santa Rosa, if you will, but you have access, if you behave, to a house in Lo Curro. So I put on my jeans, with my sweater around my waist, my blue shirt, my hair down to my shoulders, and I move comfortably around the uptown area. It's a short walk from there to the Catholic University. In the university I discover love, instructions for disassembling the father and the mother; and since I take myself seriously, I go on taking things apart and I disassemble the university and, suddenly, I'm in more pieces than I can handle; I've taken the whole damned thing apart and decide to leave, because I took it all apart and it's not worth shit. In any case I leave.

Actually, I'd rather not divulge the details. What can I say to Custodio? He is a priest who grew up in the slums and whose family still lives there. He heard it was bombed and he set out to investigate. When he saw what happened he said Mass and read the Saint James letter about the poor and the rich, Sunday the 16th of September. Who was going to listen to him? The soldiers had already been and gone and the *Carabineros* too. Even if he could have preached to the faithful they wouldn't have heard him, because in the morning with the Hawk Hunters roaring overhead, you can't hear a thing.

But I heard it and I'll let him know.

At dawn the planes went skimming over the belfry and the dry crests of the palms, an incessant thunder, echoed and amplified on the flanks of San Cristóbal hill. In bed, covered up to my nose by all the blankets I could find, practically frozen, I looked through the skylight and saw a low reddish sky with no stars, and I sensed the approaching wings of the monsters. The dog raised himself and began digging. I got up and dressed. The frost shimmered in the garden. The dog watched me. Wearing a sweater, coat and muffler, staying close to the wall, I went up to the attic next to the belfry. You can see a large part of the city from there, all the way from the river to Santa Lucía Hill, the Gran Avenida and San Miguel. Some lights, perhaps trucks, might be indicative of troop movements. But nothing is very recognizable. What I see is the sky, still dark, closing over the barren hills, a kind of shadowy wall without density or corners, an abyss, or perhaps the bottom of an abyss. I'm shivering with cold, but I don't want to go back down. Something worries me in the air that starts blowing and shakes the wet eucalyptus, something muffling the sound of shooting in the neighborhood and signaling an indefinite new danger, the echo of a tragedy that has yet to happen.

I suddenly hear a whisper in the distance, an avalanche, a dull sound, prolonged, subterranean, like a mountain tumbling down, but I can't see anything, and I have the feeling night is tearing itself open in some meadow or in the foothills of the sierra, a broad movement of earth and water, tall trees slapping into deep mud and splattering the sky, all of them crashing into a bottomless pit underneath the city, so far away and yet at the same time here, under my feet and over my head. The bells tremble, not enough to toll, vibrating in the darkness; it's the metal clapper that moves by itself, making a murmur that starts, grows and waits, like a dark tongue licking the wind.

I hear steps coming up the stairs, press my body against the ground. No one can see me. The whole floor creaks and I see a tall shadow, graceful, in profile; it's Juan, wrapped in his poncho, hair loose. Soon we are both lying flat, our faces stuck to the boards, looking through the cracks into the street. An armored car goes by and shoots—not at us—at another roof—not in Recoleta or Santos Dumont—rifle fire. They go off fast, losing themselves again in the emptiness of the wet pavement marked at intervals by the white glare of the streetlamps.

"Don't get up," Juan says, "be very careful, there're more of them on the way, and they'll be shooting."

Some fighting not far from here, small arms mostly, it's hard to say where; then comes a hail of bullets and the rattling of machine gun fire and afterwards blasts that could be cannon fire; then silence, a strange silence, growing from the nearby side streets and coming down the avenue, overwhelming us with an even more oppressive silence, in the ears, in the chest, leaving us breathless, anxiously waiting. Juan notices my shaking and hands me a cigarette. We are now sitting on the floor with our legs crossed. I search vainly for some opening in the sky, clouds, stars—nothing. I look at Juan and I feel that the act of smoking gives us the warmth of companionship in the cold mist of dawn. He understands and looks at me, and in his eyes is a bright smile: he is a white-haired, gallant priest, a man-child, hard as a dagger. I imagine his brittle teeth in the darkness, and I can see the bony fingers ritually manipulate the cigarette, tracing signs with the glowing tip and the ashes.

When the sky finally clears over the mountains, which reflect and diffuse the pearl-gray light, and even the tempestuous gray is lit from within puffing rose clouds, a strange sight surprises us and we stare at it in silence. Far away, a huge cloud of a thick ochre color is suspended, growing without rising, seeming to smooth out in the basin of the valley. It turns red, but the color is false because it seems made of transparencies inside which are reflections of reflections and the changing glow of dawn. Neither Juan nor I understand right away. In a trance we consider that sudden explosion of luminous dust in the green and white of the Andes. But the morning doesn't clear up, persisting in its tight mist, everything is still and silent. No more shots. Dawn is a sober ceremony of calm, slow lights. Only that cloud like a crimson awning stands in back of the city presiding over a ritual we will never understand.

And finally Custodio returned from saying Mass and told us that during the night the people from the settlement had ambushed and attacked a truckload of *Carabineros*; they jumped them, firing away, and then hanged two of the bodies. At dawn reinforcements arrived and planes came. They killed everyone, the women, the old people, the children, the cats and dogs. There are no young men anymore; there never were.

The red cloud stayed in the air for several days.

I must write these lines without hate. What happened is a great misfortune, but I refuse to judge anyone. The details will be known and history will arrange them. For what purpose? It is possible that this time there will be a history but no country. What will become of Chile? I mean in a few more years, several years. Those who celebrate the slaughter today, those who went out to kill with their own private pistols and revolvers, the heavy madonnas who kissed their soldiers today, will get tired and forget the meaning of all their enthusiasm. They will also die. They will have lost relatives and friends. The rictus will be that of a skull and the survivors among them will eventually protest and rebel, lose their fear, demand liberty; they will search for the tribunes and ask for elections. They will get ready for new business.

Chile will never be the same. The opposition of 1973 will be wiped out. All of them. There will be the walking and the buried, all of them dead. I don't share that hatred; I don't even know how to shoot a gun or use a knife. I will search for the believers in Christ the revolutionary, the real ones, those who decided to save themselves and conquer the purity of the tough and the brave, those who stuck the cross in the ground and made it a place of love. I know that if God leaves men suspended in the air for an eternity and looks away for a second, men will fashion a quick knife out of bone, a uniform from a shroud, and they'll slit each other's throats effectively. So we must hope, then, that God doesn't forget us.

Chileans didn't invent soldiers. We inherited them, and we carefully taught them the rules of combat and death. As children we were told: Chileans never cry. We have nothing to do with such things now; we don't see why Chileans can't cry if we've been hurt or mistreated. We've also been told the Araucanian Indians fought for their freedom for three hundred years. We weren't told, however, that after fighting off the Spaniards they met the Chilean Army.

When I took my first communion I was dressed in a sailor suit. Someone must have had some scruples because my uniform was neither white nor blue but cream, the color of the candles and flowers that surrounded the Virgin Mary next to me.

I always admired the Chilean soldiers when I went with my father and brother to more than one military parade in Cousiño Park. And I was uplifted by the proud cadets wearing their red and white plumed helmets. I eagerly waited for them to raise their stiff legs and goose-step by. And when they went by so many times that they made the ground rumble, and the leaders drew strange pictures in the air with their walking sticks, and the gun carriages and cannons rolled by, and then the snow troops and the engineers and the Marines—I would smile cheerfully, imagining how and where this baffling grownup game would end. I thought there weren't enough planes, but I didn't like them. I was always afraid one would crash either on the President, the reviewing stand or the people in the bleachers.

Yesterday two truckloads of soldiers exploded in mid-air. They got hit by sticks of dynamite thrown from an apartment building. I didn't see it but I heard the explosions.

Chile? This is Chile? The soldiers are mostly raw recruits from the provinces or draftees from the barrio slums. Most of them have relatives in the settlements on the rivers, hills and mud flats of Chile. From our building, those who threw the dynamite look equally helpless. It will be said the country split into two equal parts. But how can you divide what is indivisible? With each death of a poor child in Lo Hermida or La Legua I too die. In each peasant and each worker, dressed in fatigues or shirtsleeves, tortured or shot, I die. That man who smiles and looks like a *Carabinero* sergeant standing with a submachine gun over three youths with their faces in the mud, and the other one who clubs Victor Jara in the face with a gun butt, they are also me. And those tears on the 2nd of July in the plane that brought me and my sons, crying because I didn't know where I came from or where I was going, are now a gigantic tree of anguish that rises out of me and is buried in me.

I don't know just how much harm this has done me. It could be that the grief of today will turn into the anger of tomorrow, that I will begin to understand fear and transform it into a feeling of liberty and that I will be able to live in dignity once again. Not today. I'm ashamed of all the insignificant craziness the professionals of terror have taught me and that I carry around with me everywhere, embellishing it with a smile. I want to lock myself up and hide because I'm being hounded to death by people who talk to me about order and home and country, while they riddle my windows and shoot down my door and hunt me on every streetcorner of Chile with an iron bar ready to smash my soul.

My family, which is for the most part delighted with the triumph of the Armed Forces, would like me to think of Luz María as a woman possessed. She was indoctrinated, they say, crossing themselves. She is the one responsible for the separation, she's a vicious schemer. You gave her everything. What have you got now. Nothing. But that's not true. It is and it isn't true. In fact I did give her everything. And today I have nothing, not even the children. If Luz María destroyed me, it must be because I destroyed her. And if she saved herself it is because we will save ourselves together. I got married when I was 21, having found a road I recognized instantly. I thought I had lost my Catholic faith. I've already said that in my religious life I easily understood the Mother and the Son but never completely understood the Father. I am not given to abstractions. I would have understood it if the Father had gone up on the cross. I mean, something concrete. But the Son said he had been abandoned. It is not my wish to blaspheme, so I will go on to the rest of my testimony. I did not comprehend why my mother left my father. Today I think I know why.

I mentioned that when I landed at Pudahuel on July 2 my father was not waiting for us. I was puzzled, but I didn't hold it against him. I took the children to Luz María and gave them to her. It was obvious there was no room for me. She was relaxed but inattentive. We didn't say much. The children looked happy and did not seem overly upset. I wasn't told or asked where I was going. As I said, I left the children with her and took off. That night someone made me a bed in the living room of their apartment.

I arrived at my father's apartment July 3rd. He seemed pleased to see me and have me there. But he went out soon after. Alone, I looked at his books, his music, his pictures, everything neat and orderly, his ivories, porcelains and paintings, his somber, old-fashioned furniture, and I was thinking the present pattern revealed some intention: as if everything there were part of a trophy collection, the practical result of a methodical, understated hunt. Thus the photos of mothers and black-haired women with silky eyes, dainty mouths and dark dresses, and of long-haired boys and girls and family groups in the park, on the farm or in a room at the Club de la Unión, the diplomas and autographs, some medals and even an ancient saber in a glass case, had all been collected over the years, hung out to dry in that cold, tight room to witness not a family history, but the skill of a hunter and taxidermist. There was no portrait of my mother there. Not a single reminder. The piano was a masculine piece, like a desk or the shop of a fine carpenter.

Remembering details from years ago, intimate conversations with my mother and Marcelo, I came to the conclusion that this man of action with no acts, closed and austere, this pale, spare man, with thin lips and light eyes, who doesn't mean a thing to me, or almost nothing, once weighed all his possessions in his hands—wife, children, conflicts, resentments, uncertainty, years gone by and years to come—and decided to keep his wealth and add to it his loneliness, a special loneliness made up of things I don't know anything about and defended by unemotional principles. I say nothing of (because I don't know of) any passion. But suppose it was that way. What was behind the separation, we can only guess.

But if there were no pretext or immediate reason, is it possible that people separate in silence and move quickly away, seeking direction like cells in a microscope shaking loose in changing colors and blind dividing edges, unexpectedly? Let us suppose my mother knew that when she confronted the enigmatic solitude of the old man she was burning her bridges. Nevertheless, knowing her, I think there could be another reason: blind obstinacy, without explanation. She rebelled, she felt rejected, perhaps put down, and reacted with hardness and pride.

The point is that the three of us went to Miami, and from there—a big town white and green like a Protestant cemetery or a golf course driven by the wind, populated by straying elders and amnesiacs in Bermuda shorts—we went to Washington. First, to a boarding house at the edge of the black ghetto. My memory is of just this: a brick and mortar house, dilapidated porch, a small corner grocery and a college without established borders, vast concrete playgrounds, barracks either of wood or with tin siding, barbed wire fences, basketball nets swaying in a wind dirtied with papers and soot.

That ghetto university was like a fast-motion movie for us. The things we do and that are done to us in a foreign language don't leave an immediate trace; we only realize they happen when years later a scar suddenly shows up that won't heal or a simple emptiness that feels like nostalgia. Nothing on the surface. These empty lots fill up with buildings. The youths who run and shout slow down, dress up like adults, leave their books and binders behind, put a knapsack on their backs. Each time we come home a bit later. Or we don't come home. Our mother seems too authoritarian and domineering.

It was mandatory, anguishingly necessary for me to recover Luz María.

From the beginning, my mother had gone to work in a government office. She disappeared early in the morning, we didn't get to see her until after six in the evening. She became part of that curious crowd that emerges from cement tombs where it has enjoyed a few hours of unconsciousness, in order to enter another cement tomb, vaster and more compartmentalized, to unmake the day in a similar state of trance. Without protesting. One would say that this anonymity suited her. As if they had lifted a burden that had weighed upon her for years. She was transformed into a link of a silent chain. And with her face erased, it's possible she thought she had lost her social identity. She neither conformed nor rebelled. She simply stopped being. She never again kept track of time, which began not to transpire for her.

But it did for us. I gave up my studies and photography became a job. Marcelo continued studying and got a degree.

For a year and a half Luz María and I didn't write. We understood there was no future for us, unless we tried something drastic. If I were to return, that would solve nothing. A few months would suffice to convince me I had made a mistake. For that reason it seemed strange to me that she didn't mention coming. It seemed certain that sooner or later our relationship would land on a kind of solid ground, risky and sharp, where things connect because there is no way around it and things have our name because we were born to bear them.

However, the unexpected happened. I received a letter of hers dated from Columbus, Ohio. It looked like the missive of a missionary lost in the Amazon. Just a few lines saying she hated everything including herself. "They gave me a fellowship to learn the art of uncommunication, and I have perfected it so well that I've made myself invisible and able to walk through walls." Poor girl, I answered, come to me at once. I would send you money for the journey but I haven't any.

During it all I was thinking of the years that would pass, of the turns we would take around the world, arm in arm, as the old couples on the sidewalks in our country, coming and going with the swaying of bells, greeting familiar ghosts who, on seeing us, smile sadly saying, well, well, so here we go, and goodby.

In the end things pass, and we neither accept nor reject them because when they happen they have no reality yet. Now I'm not thinking of the details either—a little more than two years—but of a scene in a foreign film with subtitles in Spanish: Luz María dressed in gray and I in blue leaving a little white church, the lawns very green, a kind of violet light in the air, and suddenly the rain pouring down violently, densely, ourselves running, soaked, climbing into the car of a friend, and immediately the smooth noise of the tires running on the water down the narrow streets, vacant, fading out.

Some years have passed, and my children too guess. But what? How much do they know? When I left them with Luz María, they didn't seem traumatized. Maybe they were stunned. But they remember, ah! how they remember.

Luz María's first attack occurred in Washington, one

night when we were getting ready to go out to dinner. Cristiancito was three years old, Marcos two. My mother was putting them to bed. Luz María was dressing in the bedroom. I passed by the hall several times and saw her, first in her slip doing her eyebrows, then with her black dress pulled up putting on her stockings. Later that night, I would have to take my mother back to her apartment, or if she were asleep in the children's room I wouldn't disturb her. We would take off our shoes and turn out the lights. It would depend on the evening. If Luz María spoke to some older person who excited her physically and intellectually, if I went unnoticed, if when we returned we commented seriously on what had happened, and if, as I took her hand in the car, she would allow me to sink mine softly between her legs, if she would let herself be kissed, then, near the heater, we would end up undressing on our feet, silently helping each other and embracing on the rug. It seemed to me it was getting late. I looked in the bedroom and said let's go, it's past 8:00. Luz María was standing in the middle of the room and she looked at me with red eyes. Suddenly, she threw herself on the bed and started to moan. It was an absurd scene because she didn't let go of her handbag. Her face was flushed, she was gritting her teeth. I went up to touch her. She threw herself on the floor. The sounds she made were not moans, they were the cries of someone tortured inside. Pent-up anger, released slowly with increasing violence. She was tearing off her dress. I went to look for my mother. When we got back Luz María was naked, in a corner, her jaws tightly clenched. I left my mother with her to run for the phone. I called a doctor who promised to come. Hours passed. I didn't dare go back to the bedroom; I heard my mother's voice; blows, things falling. Finally the doctor's car appeared, looking for the number of our house. I went running out. I tried to explain what was happening but he wouldn't listen to me. He was a birdlike man, thin, bald, indifferent. He went in with his bag, asked where the bedroom was and locked himself up alone with Luz María. My mother came and sat with me in the living room. I couldn't make up my mind to look at her. She was pouring down a thick stream of cognac. She wasn't talking. The room started to depress me, the old furniture, the fake wood, the ticking radiators covered with asbestos bandages, the dirty ashtrays, a stiff rug like a muddy cowhide, curled at the edges. I remembered something my father once said. I thought the doctor would slap Luz María and then give her a shot that would knock out a horse. I was engulfed by a wave of tearful sympathy: I wanted to run into the room, protect her from the old man, caress her. My mother noticed, maybe, because she told me to wait, croaking from her fat throat. I paid no attention to her. I tiptoed to the bedroom. The door was still closed. I stuck my ear to it but I couldn't hear a thing. I knocked gently. In a few moments the door opened. The doctor stared at me and then turned his back. Luz María was wearing her nightgown and doing something I was hard-pressed to comprehend. She was carefully arranging all kinds of objects on the floor in a perfect line the length of the walls, and now she was moving them delicately, filling in all the gaps. Hair covered her face. Her movements were quick and sure; she didn't stop when I came in, she didn't see me. I thought the two were playing some ghastly doll game. The doctor was dropping the syringe into his bag and throwing away a piece of cotton. Seeing her, my anxiety became tears; standing next to her I began to cry. I remembered a similar scene some time ago. My mother prostrated, hysterical, stammering, and my father taking me by the hand and placing me next to her and she looking at me continuing to moan, and then I start wailing and trembling with fear, and my father saying you see, you are making the boy suffer, please calm down, but she's still crying and starts talking nonsense, looking at me with an obscene glassy stare. I want Luz María to hear me cry. I close my eyes and say a prayer. I pray for something to happen, anything. But Luz María continues her game of dolls, straightening up things that have suddenly seized her and follow her around the floor, surrounding her like tiny animals. The doctor goes out and calls. I don't want to leave her alone. Nothing will happen to her, he tells me, she'll soon be asleep. I follow him into the living room. He speaks to me without sitting down or paying any attention to my mother. I want to know exactly what happened tonight, has she gone crazy, should I call an ambulance, call her mother? He looks at me and doesn't seem to understand what I've said; he gets impatient. He hands me a paper. Begin giving her these pills tomorrow, he says and leaves. I look at my mother who is engrossed in her cognac. What do you think? I ask her. But I don't wait for an answer. I go back to the bedroom and start feeling fear and also compassion and the urge to kiss Luz María and undress her and lie by her side. She is asleep. The objects are there lined up along the wall; so I begin to create order, my order, and I take the scissors, the mirrors, the pencils, brushes, combs, tweezers, colognes, back to the bathroom, and while straightening up it seems we're back to normal, and that Luz María is all right somehow, that nothing has really happened and that everything will be forgotten tomorrow and we can start fresh and that's the last time she'll be sick. I turn off the light, close the door, return to the living room. My mother says in a low voice that Luz María will never be well again, I should get ready to live with these crises for the rest of my life, and living that way is like sleeping with a time bomb. I find a glass and pour some cognac. I don't listen to her although she keeps talking. I'll wait out the days and forget about this.

But time goes fast. It's a Saturday night and Luz María walks next to me shrieking insults; we look for the car, I'm lost on unfamiliar streets; no one is around and suddenly she throws her bracelets and rings in my face, then her shoes and her clothes and she is hurling everything at me, all she has on is her panties in the middle of the street, spitting curses and a police car appears and shines its searchlight and I hear the siren of an ambulance; a red light goes around and around in my face, and they take her away and commit her; they've injected her with an oversized syringe and the last time I see her she is walking in an empty room going around and around an imaginary well, dressed in a white gown, wrinkled, short, open in the back, and I see her long skinny legs, her back, her soft round ass; and later I'm crying on the bed of a nameless hotel, with a pillow on my face feeling violent desire between my legs.

I was turning into an unassuming tree, pruned so much I wasn't too sure of my trunk, ashen, peeling, in this airless city made of wire and streetlamps, pipes used by thugs, emergency doors for the victims that come in off the streets wet with rain and frost. Each day she spent in the sanitarium was one of bitter confrontation with myself. I was emptying, scraped with fear, short of breath, full of remorse, pretending that one morning Luz María would come back and we would start all over again. The children would be waiting for her, my mother would leave, there would be no need to remember anything, everything would be forgiven. But I would arrive at the hospital, go up in the elevator, get off on the empty corridor and sit. There was only one window guarded by thick bars and a door with no visible lock. The waiting would give me chest pains; I would walk from one end to the other without pausing, from the door to the elevator, until I heard the keys, the buzzers and the door open. The nurse would tell me the same thing every day, that Luz María did not wish to see me. Behind the nurse I could see more bars and mattresses and fences, people dressed in white and slow strollers in bathrobes. I kept up my efforts, morning and night, for two weeks. I stopped going to work and only saw the children when they were asleep. One evening the nurse blocked my way, took me to a tiny windowless room and showed me a chair. Later, angry as hell, I walked past the patients without looking at them, feeling them somehow dangerous. The doctor was an old worn-out man with a gray beard and bloodshot eyes. Why do you want her released? he asked. The children, myself, my mother, our home. He didn't hear me. She's safe here, he stammered—who will be responsible for her life if she leaves? What about love and me and my mother and the children? The doctor thrust out his palm as if to shield himself. It's a mistake: it will be your responsibility. I don't care, I said vehemently. This is a prison. Where are you taking her? I knew he had a dirty mind. I hated him, but said nothing. He took me to Luz María's room. She was curled up on her bed. With her white crazy gown. Her face was hidden between her arms and she just kept crying. We were there all afternoon. She cried while I stood against the wall. In the evening my mother came and between the two of us we dressed her, picked up her things and took her away. The door closed behind us like a safe.

And it opened again. Three months later. When I came home from work, I locked myself up for hours in the darkroom to develop the photographs I'd taken that day. I was vaguely listening to the voices of the children. Afterwards, the silence somehow crept into the closet and worried me. I quickly put away the film, turned on the light and went out. I suppose the red color of the safelight followed me and when Luz María saw me she was frightened. I went to check on the children. They were asleep. I went back to the living room and she looked at me. I must have turned pale and I felt like kneeling next to her and crying. But it was too late. She was talking about the children and she moaned. I tried to caress her and she slapped me. Then she began to throw things to the floor very slowly and deliberately. She was smashing glasses, pictures, books; she went around the room meticulously destroying, passing over certain things, until she came to the window and I saw she was about to throw herself through it. I grabbed her by the arms and we began to wrestle. The children were awake and crying. I was alone with her, I couldn't leave her and go to the phone and call my mother. Luz María was very strong in spite of her skinny arms and lanky legs. She had me on my back on the floor with her knee in my stomach. After a struggle I was able to free myself and push her off. She got up in a leap and ran to the children. I followed her without knowing what to do. She got them out of bed and now the three of them were yelling and running. He is going to kill us, she screamed, he is going to kill us. And they followed her, with me behind at an absurd trot, because I didn't want to catch her, and couldn't think of anything to say to them. We ran like this around the apartment for I don't know how long. The children were lying on the floor now. Luz María moaned leaning against the wall. She had a big knife and her hand was bleeding. I went to the phone. I yelled out our address to the operator and asked for an ambulance and the woman asked me a stupid question. I left the phone off the hook and stood there in front of Luz María, shaking. We spent some time like that. The children on the floor, she moaning, with her fingers gripping the handle of the knife. The ambulance was on its way blasting sirens and screams and whistles. The door of the apartment swung open and they came in and found us that way, a frozen scene on the screen, and they strapped her to a stretcher and took her away, and I put the children to bed and then began to pick up the broken glass and saw my hands were covered with blood. When my mother came a policeman was writing down my mumblings.

Then I seemed to see a flowering tree in Forestal Park, an almond tree, a kind of staff or candelabrum or cage, or all three at the same time, and inside the tree a fine rain was falling, incomprehensible, because everything around it was radiant, and the sun hovered over the tree like a silk umbrella, and we stared at it surprised and happy. She cried and I cried too. I was asking her to marry me and kissing her hands. Luz María was saying no; it had nothing to do with caring, or anything relating directly to me. She just wanted to leave, that's all. Later she kissed my eyes and forehead and smiled when she saw me cry. I was trying to understand, but fleeting images were distracting me. I saw more lights coming off her and surrounding me—I wanted to delve into her through her eyes—they were like pools of very calm water, deep and softly green—I could dive into them, throw rocks into them and the surface wouldn't shatter and no waves would arise, everything would be the same, impassive, distant. At the same time, I knew with absolute certainty that Luz María and I had walked together for many years, and that age united us like two pieces of furniture, let's say two chairs, and around us there were children and deaths and other births and other deaths; there didn't seem to be any need to live those years together because they had already been lived; what was missing were some happy evenings together, some more suffering, and that hopelessness that relatives wear when we get together to celebrate anniversaries.

I don't know why Luz María acted superior to me all the time. She would say no and then would say love. Outside, in the park, a steady rain; on the window a thin stream of drops, like blood, and the water dribbling down the hoods, roofs and windows of cars and onto the ground, like rice; Luz María in her overcoat, with her back to me; I wear a suit, tie, hat and shoes. I kiss her.

It was the first time we discussed a separation. The family said it was hysteria and a trick. The doctor said deep depression.

Luz María's mother sent a message: let her come back with the children: she's not about to become the cook and the nursemaid, not only for the children but also for that idiot she married. She ought to come home, she is anemic, she probably doesn't get enough to eat, she should be with her own kind and leave that moron—annul the marriage.

Luz María, serene, silent, smothered the children with attention, actually seeming to be afraid of me. My mother said she ought to leave and added that in her state she shouldn't travel with the children. Her idea prevailed. I thought it was unjust, cruel, for her and for me. Luz María couldn't be separated from us. I admit what I felt was probably irresponsible, a childish effort to erase everything, still believing that she, in her straight jacket, would continue to love me. Something like breaking a crystal glass and thinking that, with time, the cracks and the glued pieces won't be noticed. I knew I had hurt her and left deep scars, that she would shatter in my hands whenever I touched her.

As it turned out, I would recognize the truth much later, in September and October of '73.

One afternoon coming home from work I had the sensation everything was about to end, and I was moving on a greased slide, falling in a tango I'd prepared for a long time, not very worried, but taking all kinds of precautions. I was alone, filling up days like holes with things that didn't matter.

I worked as a photographer in a Panamerican organization. With a camera hanging around my neck like a scapular, I went from one social function to another, shooting sea lions and penguins with a glass in hand, visiting politicians, painters, concert artists, singers. I had no fixed working hours. I moved at will through the city, and I could easily pass any afternoon aboard a huge barge, dressed up as a floating restaurant, drinking white wine, swayed by the dirty waves of the river that little by little became covered with a wide, changing fire, until it faded in the twilight.

The nights were nasty attacks against Luz María. I would wake her up with my elbows and hips, tear off the sheets and attack her from all sides. Then I would go out in my shirtsleeves, with no shoes, to roam the cold green streets, through the empty avenues, the dark parks, searching for a tree that would hold my weight, but it wasn't possible, and then I would come back and hide on the sofa and lull myself to sleep with plans for revenge, in minute detail, and when I finally dropped off to sleep, I would see myself groping for a rope, making a knot, putting it around my neck and then leaping: imagining those things settled me down, they sweetened the night for me. Then I would pray and go straight to sleep.

I would go away, as I've said, and come back. Luz María didn't want to see me. I saw in her expression someone drowning in bed, crushed and beaten with a big fish, hastening the shivers that get more and more annoying and painful. She told me I cried in my sleep; I told her that I would kneel and beg her to go with me to church and make a vow; for me to go away and for her to forget me. It was the most ridiculous conversation that ever took place. I told her that I didn't want to run her life. She said my mother should stop calling her. She swallows me, she said. I thought of a boa. I told her yes, I would tell her. It doesn't matter, she added.

That midnight, when I walked into the apartment, I tried not to make any noise. The light in the hall was off, the lights in the living room were on and so were the ones in the bedrooms, the bathrooms and the kitchen, and in the middle of the living room I saw Luz María standing there naked with the children, who were also naked, the window was wide open. The drapes were billowing in the icy wind, the children were trembling, tight-lipped, looking at me. Then Luz María ran out on the small balcony and climbed onto the railing, balancing herself with her arms outstretched to a black sky full of stars, with tree-crowns below and time telescoping in on that instant. I rushed and tackled her around the waist and lowered her to the floor: she was stiff as a board, her eyes closed, gritting her teeth. Then I put the children to bed.

If one learns to talk and listen to trees, one also learns to save the body we would crush between our legs. This is a fact. In front of my window there is a maple with a thick, dark trunk, an abstract structure in the cold night of Santiago, and it has begun to reveal to me a lace of infinite delicacy, framed in branches of red and green leaves. I know it holds the world's most fiery copper in its heart and that the time will come when that copper will glow for me with enough sun to fill a courtyard. And next to it, another tree curls its yellow leaves like fingertips, and it doesn't bend with the wind or water. Under them there is a delicate azalea with four red flowers and some ferns drooping in the rain and stones darkening with moss. This is a world that exists for me and makes me feel better in the morning and comes to bed with me at night with its murmur and damp smell. I can touch it and it will come alive in my hands, as if my blessing signalled some necessary communion. I thank God for the pink and white petals flying in the rain, for the bronze buttons ready to explode on the peach, almond and cherry trees by my house, for the needles and red stars of the quince, for the birds playing in the grass and fluttering their wings in the water. Today, Luz María in my arms, naked, burning on the open bed, inventing new ways of touching, surrendered in a lost battle, waving her hands, smiling for no reason, eyes closed, she reacts as I brush her with my hands and lips and, suddenly, the whole garden is drifting, the branches rustle, the clouds brighten—if there were a sun it would be blinking—while we soar up and down, an eternal day, nameless and dateless, with her hair in my mouth and my fingers on her back, giving thanks, thanks for having suffered with her, for being saved with her, standing over the frame of a cool death, already understanding the ancient scripture, jumbled-up, chaste, sweaty, the covers all over the floor.

Today? When is today? Now I see myself alone. Through the immense skylights of the closed stadium I will see the pine forest, the rocks, the monument to the Virgin; again there doesn't seem to be any way out for me; the blue aura of the afternoon will never reach me because they closed the iron gates and locked the chains and decisive walls rose between me and that world of people who were once mine. I will look at my hand shaking, cover myself with the blanket I've brought from the cell, pray and hear the silence all around me telling me that what was begun will be completed and no one or nothing will change what is already written; and I am not too sad or hopeless because I don't know what role I'll play in what's left of the day—or the night, which for me and many others may never begin.

It's not possible, naturally, to remember all the details with accuracy, nor do they matter now, except to figure out what happened and why.

For example, a dinner at the home of a government official. We got into a political discussion. The host, redfaced and fat, burly with bloodshot eyes, fiercely attacked an important leader of the Popular Unity who wasn't present. The man's wife not only supported him but added what she considered damning testimony like: "I know this guy and, personalities aside, he behaves like a snake in the grass." A small young man with erect posture and a triangular face got into the argument to defend the absent leader. I liked his attitude, not his ringing voice or his phony radio-announcer style of delivery. I didn't get into the discussion because, besides being reticent, I was not in the mood to discuss Chilean politics. What was happening in Chile could also be the beginning of something for me, an open road, without words, but full of action. They were speaking about deficiencies, omissions, incompetence, superficialities. They appointed this man knowing all his life he behaved like a Christian Democrat. Representative of the Popular Unity! What kind of revolution is this that keeps reactionaries in influential positions? They were really talking about jobs. Who had been appointed and who hadn't! What did I care about that?

Outside, on the terrace, a boy with dark hair and a bird's face was strumming a guitar. In the shadow of ferns, leaning against logs, long-haired girls and boys were listening; smooth shadows, graceful, with the carefully concealed chic of Providencia. If upstairs old men wasted saliva attacking the distribution of appointments, down here the world kept up its stream of upper-class chitchat. What dream did these youngsters defend against their fathers—the old guard, armed with bolts and master keys, who deceived themselves into thinking they'd engineered a change that could not, would not, alter anything? Upstairs the old men would screw their new model together; downstairs the young men, skeptical, unexcited, made jokes, unscrewed it. Each old man dressed up as a guerilla, with a glass of whiskey in his hand, had his sweet, long-haired child below, elegantly stirring the fire of the soft Chilean middle class. Upstairs: institutionalized revolution. Downstairs, the kids boasting about rich relatives and exchanging memories of fancy summer resorts, all the time defending the affected alienation of the Mapocho hippies. This low-key concert of gutless tunes was drowning out the grumblings of the tap-dance revolution upstairs. I wasn't involved with them because I had already outgrown the vacation period of my life.

But who told you every Chilean is a revolutionary? We are conservative by birth. We have a name and a past to conserve. The middle class doesn't ever want a revolution. You don't say. Reform, yes, because we know what the *roto* is worth, and once in a while it's necessary to stop the bastards who take advantage of him. Don Eduardo Frei hit the nail on the head: revolution is spelled with dollars. He got more votes than Miss Universe.

That kid knew all the Quilapayún songs and he wanted to sing the Santa María Cantata. But the other kids were requesting "When the tortilla flips and the poor have bread, the rich will eat shit." I especially remember a fat girl, a kind of barmaid with blond braids, singing loudly, "Is it the tomato's fault?" And her father, with a German name but married to a pedigreed Basque, was listening to her ecstatically, looking at his colleagues, proud of his dumpling, owner of an inviolate farm, a revolutionary untouched by agrarian reform. We were all singing and the "sons-of-bitches" of the song lifted up our hearts. That's the way we got along downstairs; upstairs the argument got more heated. One of the orators left by himself. He had no sooner gone than they were already shouting at him: counterrevolutionary, imperialist, Frei-lover.

Those people impressed me that night for two reasons: they saw something in me that wasn't there, and Luz María did not seem to exist for them. I don't know if in some way I seemed powerful. It must have been my way of not saying much, just watching, with a shock of hair over my eyes, immobile, or the way others passed by my side, over me, through me, without noticing.

Luz María, upstairs, was in a corner alone, smoking. I am sure she she hadn't spoken to anyone. I stayed with her as in so many other times, not knowing what would happen later, if her way of looking at me was hard or empty, but knowing she saw everything, without seeing or hearing, like a delicate screen that receives images from a distance, an open eye that captures the red and black spots, an exposed film with blurred people caught in the act of crying or trying to escape.

How wrong one can be! I said "without seeing or hearing" ... how could I know whether she saw or not and if what she was listening to would not come and hit us in the teeth with the weight of a stone?

By fragments of letters and conversations that I'm reviewing, I realize now what pathetic heights my blindness reached. I analyzed her, classified her and prescribed with impunity, without stopping to think that she could return the favor, analyzing me in turn, classifying me and writing me off. But things didn't really happen this way. Here is a sample from a letter she wrote before coming from Chile:

"There are certain things which, seemingly, touch you and leave no mark; one would say you lack the patience to assimilate the possible ways of understanding a fact or a person and that you are more comfortable with a hasty conclusion, even knowing you are making a mistake. At times weak-kneed, static, squeezing tightly everything that gives you intellectual pleasure because it inflates and elevates you; other times you launch yourself forth with childish impatience. You don't keep step, or stay level. You walk along a road you think has been made for you, without noticing that it's made or unmade for you at the whim of other people. You enjoy being spoiled. And hate to be judged. If they criticize you, you cower, if they don't you feel upset. You don't want to be left out."

In conversation she was less eloquent but much more to the point. I remember one day when we talked about violence. "What's important," she said, "is to be able to feel it as something which involves you personally. Never as an abstraction. Nor as an accident."

"I hate violence," I answered in the voice of a holy man.

"One does not hate violence," she responded, "You either defeat it or fall in front of it. It can't be eluded. You might run away, if you like. But that doesn't mean you've avoided it. You have yielded to those who practice it. If you confront it, you are already involved. You prefer never facing the alternatives. And this is impossible. The whole world does violence to you, all the time. The only reasonable thing to do is to know how to muster your resistance, because then you can accommodate to circumstances and, however hopeless you may feel, come out on top."

During the time she suffered her depressive crises, I neither understood nor imagined what her problems could actually be. It's easy to say along with all the old relatives, aside from parents and close friends, that a person goes through a "change of life," even at the wrong age, and that you should adapt yourself, sacrifice yourself, cope with it. It will pass, it will pass, they say and leave you with a time bomb under your bed. Change of life for these people is like a change of hat. One day you decide you don't like this head with which you entered the world, and poof! you change it for one more comfortable, tranquil and, if possible, more attractive. Besides, this formula is applied to old ladies, young matrons and odd sorts, eternal adolescents. It's very possible Luz María confronted in herself an image of growing uselessness and a feeling of helplessness, the result of her rejection of that which for me had become routine. For example, that flat and ambiguous environment into which we had fallen ought to have been repugnant to her: a bare church with a flag on the pole, with clerics that speak like policemen or insurance brokers, uniformed neighbors who speak a language made to order for the daily pot in which the whole family is cooked. For years we lived in a world that literally had four walls and no window. Through ignorance, through our own incapacity? It was necessary to rebel. But how? One can also fall into such a world by one's own desperate decision, preferring to join the band of the alienated.

Likewise, it is very probable that Luz María was changing by leaps and that no one—myself less than anyone—understood the sense of these leaps. Withdrawn, remote, she could seem indifferent and even hostile. Perhaps she felt rejected and thus rejected in turn. About the old Lutheran ladies—conservative and anti-Black, anti-Mexican, anti-Asian, anti-everything with more color than a soda cracker—she said:

"If they lived in Chile, they would hate the *rotos*. It

hurts them to see themselves reflected in the misery and ignorance which they help to create because it is the only thing they know how to manage and maintain to defend themselves. Speak to them of charity and you make them happy. Tell them they have to divide up the land and now they want to crucify you."

When she went back to Chile, I don't know what part of her "change" she could communicate to the people who, for a long time, had been popping the little balloons of pious charity. A new breed of person went out on the streets and to the shantytowns and the countryside to speak of agrarian reform, of a church with a social conscience, and of immediate action. If a Catholic decided to act in Chile, he always had the Christian Democracy to divide up, to separate another little wing from, slightly more revolutionary.

It's too easy to be a hypocrite writing about these things. What have I said? That in destroying her I was passing from one phase of pretense to another, covering that hairy zero I was, feeling important yet weightless, like a monk full of hot air, or like those phony Buddhas who dance, sing and slap their tambourines wrapped in lemon-colored sheets in front of the Bank of America. At least they run the risk of being mocked by the passersby. I, on the other hand, disguised as I don't know what, took pictures lacking charm or strength, talked about making movies, maybe a picture about the moment when the world grows up, sweet Chile's menopause, perhaps. Everything was timeless but also day-to-day; I would pile up and sweep away the days trying to make the sidewalk in front of my empty shop disappear. I was bothered by the place that was growing around me. I was fattening up inside and getting soft and would often drip because crying helped me keep the doors open.

I've said, or perhaps I haven't said, that at a given moment everything snapped shut on me. There was no longer any exit. It was when I stopped going to work and didn't look for another job. I became afraid of Luz María. I thought I still had the children left. For what? They were part of the pretense. The children in reality belonged to their grandparents, to a world that refused to grow up and would win the game in the end, because these problems are not for sentimentalists like me. But it's easy to say "case closed." Through inertia I would bang my head not against something I considered closed but what I wrongly considered open. I was still looking for a way. There may have been an element of predestination. Marcelo knew we were entering a tunnel and he saw a little light, as they say, at the other end. I saw neither tunnel nor light but yielded to the movement that he and others were creating around me. I don't want to give an impression of indifference or apathy. My decision was firm: to return to Chile at that moment signified a new intent to find peace along with Luz María and the conviction that events were finally going to give meaning to what, until then, was a shabby chain of attempts and failures.

Besides, I had immediate work. I haven't mentioned that in 1971, when Allende was in New York, I came to know him personally, since I was commissioned to prepare a photographic record of his speech before the UN Assembly. I showed him my work and he liked it. During a conversation while walking—all the photographers following him down Fifth Avenue—he accepted my idea of doing a few interviews and taking a lot of pictures, which could be published in the form of a book. This and my future plans for a film on the changes in Chile supplied a practical reason to what could have seemed a new plan for adventure.

Several things did not fit into my plans, however, and I didn't even think about them: the days I was to live with my father; also, will children just disappear?

I don't want to dominate or destroy anyone. I must find individuals to be with now, not clinging vines. I have to live with a conscience—perhaps not clear yet, but gradually getting lighter—and learn not to coerce anyone: that conscience will grow and give me a sense of strength not in the defeat of others but in discovering their strength. I call on God now more than ever, not out of piety but respect for everything that comes my way, negative or positive, because in each confrontation I may find harmony and, if things go well for me, I might find peace.

There were, naturally, many loose ends to tie up. I am not, all things considered, anything but a 27-year-old individual, whose marriage went on the rocks, as they say, because of his own insufficiency and cowardice, and who now looks for a balance sheet, not to show off what he has earned, but rather because the moment has come to begin another account in earnest.

I came back to the San Borja Towers. There was nothing to be afraid of. My father was known by the ladies and gentlemen of "Fatherland and Liberty" in the building and the neighborhood. He kept his dignity, closed himself to every discussion, expressed himself strictly with bare truths. Allende? Finished, his days were numbered. The military? What's the matter with them? Why don't they do something more drastic? He didn't mean the truckers or the terrorists or the black market profiteers. Chaos with a capital letter that the Armed Forces, also in caps, must remedy. He never asked for our opinion. He spoke and we listened. Besides, he only spoke when necessary. He read *El Mercurio* holding the newspaper with a steady hand. He would study me with his little blue eyes, adjusting the knot in his tie. He would ask for tea with milk, but there is no tea. He would stay there lost in thought, look at his watch, go out on the balcony. He would come in again, listen to the radio.

The San Borja Towers, standing out above the fog, seemed to face each other in silent challenge. Across the Alameda, the iron UNCTAD, red and black, dripped with the morning dew. The chimneys spewed their thick smoke into the center of town. A neon sign in front of Plaza Baquedano was blinking. The Tajamar Towers, far off, faded into the whiteness of the mountains.

Below, I saw a gray Opel go slowly by with its lights on, the blue-suited driver had a pistol on the seat beside him; I had the impression he was patrolling, which seemed absurd.

I saw people walking downtown. I didn't see much activity in the other towers. I went into the living room. My father had dressed. The telephone rang. He said hello with a cutting voice and then listened. Ah, yes, he said, it's about time. No, sure, who'd be fool enough to go out, do what must be done, stay at home and wait, I will call you in the afternoon, could be, but not lunch, this might last longer than you think, at night for sure, but I'll call you.

Over in the eastern Towers there are a lot of Cubans, Brazilians, Argentinians, Bolivians. They must have left by now for the industrial belts, the workers' settlements. My father was looking at me with a smile. The doorbell rang. It was the accountant from across the hall. He was pale, his hair on end, stammering in a loud voice. My father did not ask him in. He had just arrived from downtown. Doors and windows must be closed and cars put in the garage. The bullets, sir, everywhere, nothing will be left of the Communists. The country's been saved, my friend, they're going to get the shit kicked out of them. Have your flag ready because I'll pick you up and we'll celebrate in Plaza Bulnes, in La Moneda, you understand? We'll go in my car. My father tried to calm him down. The accountant with his empty blue eyes waved his arms repeating the news about Valparaiso and Puerto Montt. When he left, my father turned on the radio again. The pronouncements of the Junta had begun, at first they sounded like commercials—maybe it was the professional announcers—telling about the coup and passing on orders for the population of Santiago. Be calm and stay at home, was the announcement. The accountant, who had a window facing the Alameda, was unfurling his flag. The neighbors from the adjacent Tower looked on in silence. Suddenly, the traffic changed direction, the cars began speeding toward Providencia. I could see them go by smooth and shiny as if directed by remote control. The janitor locked the doors of our building with chains. I phoned my brother. He didn't answer. There was something chillingly routine about the way the radios kept announcing the military coup. Voices with no sign of alarm said the war had been won, that calm reigned throughout the country, that the Junta had assumed power and the decrees of the new government would be broadcast soon. Nothing was said about Allende.

I had the impression that a perfect net had fallen over the country, nobody seemed surprised, in a few hours we would peacefully sit down to lunch under a government of law and order, innundated by meat, bread, oil and detergent falling from the sky. I picked up my camera, threw my green jacket over my shoulder and said goodby to the old man. He stared at me in surprise. Again? But he did not lose his smile. Even that goodby was going to be routine. I went down the elevator alone and asked the janitor to open the iron gates. You are taking a risk for nothing, he said, because there isn't going to be any celebration, and besides, it looks dangerous downtown. Can't you see how all the cars are heading up for Providencia? You'll have a hell of a time getting back. Bye, I said and began walking down the Alameda to the Plaza Bulnes. The UNCTAD, closed and empty. At the doors of the Catholic University I noticed small groups of young people in earnest conversation. Nearing the Santa Lucía I saw the first amored cars. No one stopped me or questioned me. The stores were all closed. I saw people heading towards Forestal Park. I arrived at the church of San Francisco. Now people were running. A woman was standing in the middle of the Alameda. A car stopped, the guy opened the door and she got in. I walked faster. Nearing San Antonio I heard the sound of engines behind me. I began taking pictures. It was a detachment of tanks speeding toward La Moneda. At a newspaper stand a man wrapped in a long scarf was drinking tea and listening to his transistor radio. I approached and heard the voice of Allende. I couldn't quite make out what he was saying. He seemed to be calling on the workers to occupy the factories. He said to be calm. Everybody was asking for calm. The tanks were disappearing. Be alert, Allende said. It's Radio Magallanes, the man explained, it's the only one left. Aren't you afraid I asked him. Of what he said. All hell is going to break loose. Nothing is going to happen, everything is under control. Who says? People began running by. It was a curious situation, those who had already gone to work were fleeing home while others, also running, were going into the public buildings, closing the windows and doors. I came to the corner of Morandé and the Alameda. The tanks had taken positions. I saw how the infantry soldiers arrived in trucks and established their combat posts. I watched these military maneuvers, the machine guns and bazookas, without understanding what was really happening; it was like an early morning game followed by the symphonic changing of the guard for the tourists staying at the Hotel Carrera. I was stopped by a patrol who aimed their machine guns at me. For the first time that morning I saw helmets instead of faces: I felt those machine guns could fire on their own. I went on Amunátegui and came back down Moneda. In front of the palace I could see groups of newspapermen and photographers. I couldn't get very close to any of them. Everything seemed absurd. A reporter from the Catholic University was talking into his cassette machine, while another was taking pictures of the troops; the natty journalists were observing everything attentively, but not terribly worried; television cameras dominated the street, and meanwhile, something, the net I mentioned before, was tightening, and someone was tying the last loose ends together deliberately, calmly, and in all that skill you knew the perfectly foreseeable outcome.

Suddenly, Allende appeared on the balcony of his office. Incredible. He looked towards the Plaza and with a smile waved to a group of civilians who applauded him. What can possibly happen if things like this occur? General Prats will arrive, orders and counterorders will be given, heels will click, they will salute, the tanks will go back to their barracks and Comrade President will give a speech on nationwide TV. Allende remained on the balcony for a few seconds, calm, in his well-tailored tweed jacket with a red handkerchief sprouting from its pocket. Then he went into his office and the shutters of the balcony were closed. And while this was happening, or perhaps a little later, but not much, a young man in a white sweater, with long blond hair, began setting up a machine gun on another balcony of La Moneda. He was doing it very slowly, checking everything out, aiming toward the tanks. The palace guard remained at its post. Civilians arrived on foot and by car. I recognized several ministers and leaders of the Popular Unity. There was a little commotion when a *Carabinero* general walked into the Palace. The towering guards with their shiny boots and glittering spurs whipped off salutes as the general straightened his cap and smoothed his uniform. Someone at my side said that Allende was on the radio again, saying goodby to the people. He's leaving. It was hard to believe. But so was everything else. Now civilians were exiting.

Later, at the Ministry of Defense, I saw Orlando Letelier, very pale, the knot of his tie twisted, his jacket open, surrounded by soldiers with their guns trained on him. Taller than they, he didn't look like a prisoner but more like someone guiding them to the car they drove him off in.

Shortly after, two tanks came into view and carried out a maneuver that baffled me, as if they were making a mistake: one parked in front of the main door of La Moneda, screeching to a stop. The other one remained next to the Social Security building, backed up, and went down forward again and stopped a little sideways, sort of aiming at the window of the President's office. The palace guard was now leaving in single file, some with handkerchiefs in the air signaling surrender, and they ran towards the underground parking lot on Morandé Street.

I don't know precisely when the shooting started, but it was a fierce crossfire, as if the entire Plaza de la Constitución had blown up because of some internal, invisible explosion—knocking down walls, splintering doors, breaking windows, iron fences, filling cars full of holes. In the confusion I dove under a cement bench and saw the newsmen dash down Morandé and Moneda, and men and women appeared in the doorway of the ministries with their hands in the air, and the soldiers received them with the muzzles of their guns, throwing them on the ground, questioning some, punching others, while bullets ricocheted off the buildings. Then they quickly loaded them into the military trucks and left.

I tried to take pictures and I saw a broken image in the

viewfinder: a young face at one moment complete and seconds later dissolving as if made of rubber, being erased, what was once a face opened grotesquely, slowly, its edges became lips and disappeared or blended into the red sky, full of smoke. The ground was also opening. The tanks were blasting away with their cannons. And then I saw my own eye, wide open, without lashes, dripping blood, nothing else.

Before it's too late I've got to think about certain things and search for the motives behind this sudden hell. Chile has burst open like a tree already consumed by termites. Only the bark is left. I'm not just talking about the hatred that wedges between us, because there was always hatred, but also the pretense and teachery.

Neither my parents, myself or my brother ever had fat bank accounts or mansions. But the family still has land and relatives—lots of relatives—and in spite of Marcelo and me, they count us among the families of the old bourgeoisie. So I know, then, that if a long conflict began to dissolve the family, I wasn't touched directly or very deeply. I was someone else's problem. I don't think my mother had much to do with it either, a woman of strong character and Teutonic will, but it must have affected my father at some time and left him permanently marked.

The disgust the affluent middle class feels for the poor is in my opinion a very stupid sign of ignorance. The truth is that Chileans are terribly provincial. All of them live at the end of the world in a country hemmed in by mountains and the ocean, crumbling to pieces with earthquakes and natural disasters—what agrarian reform experts refer to as "erosion." We look around us and smile. We are a homogenous people derived from a lovely European immigration. It seems the climate cooperates with the racial currents and preserves the rosy cheeks, light hair, good legs and even dissipates the persistent swarthiness that undeniably runs in our blood from the Araucanian and the mestizo. The average Chilean is intelligent, affable, overflowing with solutions, domineering yet charming. When he becomes unbalanced by poverty or laziness, he resorts to his cunning, and his cunning destroys him. He becomes a marginal person. Our pride and violent patriotism give us an air of solid consanguinity. Inbreeding. No one can interfere with us. Our affairs are straightened out by Chileans in Chile. At home. This is all part of the Chilean religion. We can accept aid from anyone, always asserting our independence and individualism. Nothing shook our middle class so much as the editorials in *El Mercurio* about political exiles during Allende's government, revolutionaries changing the pace of life in Santiago. That is why the Armed Forces began their national reconstruction by liquidating the foreigners.

Ercilla, the epic poet, called us a "fertile chosen province." He called us a "province" and he added "chosen"! This is the formula that has best defined us throughout history. We live inwardly, cultivating the particular, believing we don't really need to know the world, only ourselves—all we have to do is accept ourselves as peculiarly provincial to define our destiny. This concept must have worked well when the Basques, French and English were laying foundations in the provinces. Not so well with the "bold" Castillians and even less with the unpredictable Andalucians. A homogenous Chile (the Basque merchants, the German mathematicians, zoologists and botanists and the English accountants) asks itself what could possibly divide the family. The solid middle class has never set the pace in our country, its duty is to follow and to adjust. The peons don't count and never have counted, nor do the Araucanians, whom Chile fought against for years. Those who are shocked that the Armed Forces in 1973 have declared a "state of internal war" against a sector of Chileans forget the frontier wars against our Indians and the military actions taken to suppress the nitrate workers or the miners of Lota.

Today I observe Chileans who want a strongman and cry for more, much more blood. I don't recognize them. I understand them, naturally, but I don't know who they are. I'm not talking about criminals. I see mature people, who defend their business or trade, demand vengeance and expect it to be summary. They look at what they have lost under Allende and decide on a brutal recovery. If they are industrialists, they want the gringos to come back, credit made available and profit from foreign exchange; if they are professionals they ask for the heads of the Marxists and tell the poor to stay in their place and not bother them. There is a large foreign middle class here. I notice the presence of another sector that is not easy to define but quite recognizable; upper-class, educated abroad, hard and definite ideology, tactics of deliberate action. These are the civilians behind the armed dictatorial offensive. Their terrorism, complex and efficient, is quite sophisticated. First-rate CIA. But they look down their noses at the Brazilians as much as they do at the gringos, some for racial motives and others for reasons of class: the *norteamericano* can never hope to be graceful at anything; he might be powerful and skilled, but cultured he is not.

Following these groups is the nation: the ladies and gentlemen of the National Reconstruction, the boys and girls with bucket and brush in hand obliterating history from the walls of Chile.

Until two in the afternoon, more or less, on the 11th of September, 1973, this was the country Salvador Allende ruled.

Now I remember his white mustache—just like when I met him—he was a bit familiar and informal, a bit on his statesman's pedestal, declaiming phrases for history, and, most of the time, at a distance, alone, tremendously alone and cornered, without exit, at the mercy of his enemies, each one with a finger on the trigger, ready to shoot.

The first time I interviewed him was in his house at Guardia Vieja.

We are seated, looking at each other, I'm trying to see what these months have done to him, new wrinkles and more white hairs, more pounds—less confidence? And the cheerful face before me starts to smile. A tray appears and on it a truly holy image, a luminous, sky-gold, country-light, cool bottle of white wine, with olives and cheese, and as we drink the vineyards bloom again in the mouth and that burning cold that slides out of the mountains through the lush pepper trees seeking a calm sun.

"Why you've come I don't know," Allende tells me, "but I admire your faith. *Salud.*" "I've come to learn," I say. "It's not a time to take account of things," he says. "No, I know." Tencha, his wife, is listening to something else. She has asked me a question but she doesn't expect an answer. A tray swoops by me and stops too close to my shoulder. I've arrived feeling somewhat insecure. The front garden mingles with the one next door. Besides, Guardia Vieja is a one way street. But, the trees, the vines, the grass, the sleepy midday are reassuring, and I wait quietly on the terrace, sunning myself, letting myself be covered with hairs by a huge swaying dog, like a yellow and white silk curtain, who beats me with his tail as he passes.

Seated at the table I soon realize that Allende and his wife have a secret agreement, things that unite them and clearly distinguish them. Her smile worries me because it is not directed at anyone in particular; it keeps her aloof. I think I notice a certain tension at the table. But it could be me, not them. Things and people whisk by me quickly. Now Allende takes me into his library and stares at me from behind thick glasses. He jokes, offers cigars he brought back from Cuba. I'm glad to see him happy, healthy and strong. This time he tells me nothing. I shoot some pictures, look around. I would like to ask questions, but decide to wait.

The next time we are at the Presidential mansion on the coast at Viña del Mar. He comes up to me wearing a white guayabera, with a glass in his hand, smiling, hair neatly combed. I look at him and he seems thinner now, harder and even taller. His enemies say he walks like that, leaning backwards, because of his bulletproof vest. His open shirt reveals the white hairs on his reddish skin, burnt by the sun. We go out into the garden. The sea, the wind, the trees, the sky, whisper with the movement of summer over the hills of Viña del Mar. We have come out from a glassed-in veranda, walking among wicker furniture into the sun which rolls around searching for its favorite spot among the rocks and skyscrapers; there is that frothy background of algae and seaweed, flashing red, yellow or green between gigantic waves and tiny boats.

Let's go up to the balcony and look, he invites me, and we lock ourselves in a midget elevator that goes up creaking like an old basket. We get out in an unfinished room, without furniture, only sawhorses, hammers and nails, saws, jack planes, brushes and cans everywhere. This is the chimney, he says, and there are some charcoal lines drawn on the wall, and the desk will go here, and he points out the space next to the window, and the bookshelves will be where a ladder stands full of spattered glue and paint, and this is the balcony. Actually, we stand in the air, above Cerro Castillo, in front of the shadow of the sea and the bobbing lights, before a bright Valparaiso, in the cold wind that seems to lift the silhouettes of the fig trees and the flowery propellers of quince and hawthorn, with the blue eucalyptus swaying in the background.

The President tells me thirty children from the fishing villages of Arauco are vacationing in Cerro Castillo Palace, chosen for good grades in school. Go see them, he urges me, and I go and have breakfast with them. They are the same small urchins of my childhood, beautiful pink and brown children, dark page boys, with wide mouths, thick eyebrows, tender and lively eyes. They approach Allende as a grandfather, they embrace him and take his hand. He asks them where they are going today and they answer to the candy factory. Those who wait on their tables are sailors, and I like that conviviality in the Chilean tradition, that warm bread in the morning of palms and pines at Cerro Castillo. We all go out into the garden. An army helicopter approaches and hovers over us causing a storm of leaves and seeds. It descends and settles in the grass. The President comes out looking very well-groomed and elegant, followed by his military aides; he stops in the doorway and waves goodby; the children chant his name. The dragonfly rises over the trees, hovers for a moment and then veers off sideways, spiralling like a kite.

Another image. Now we are very far away from each other. Something separates us that turns into a red sky, and tonight Allende is just a voice, an arm, a head, on a crowded balcony, with a sky full of smoking torches and thousands of flags. I'm so far away that I've missed the speech. I look at my friends and talk about his family and the years that have passed and the years to come, the distances in the pampas, the speeches in the echoing warehouses and the coal pits, the demonstrations and counter-demonstrations.

Suddenly I think of the President lying on a bed that does not yet exist but already awaits him, in a disordered room, spent shells on the floor, plaster heads on the muddy rug and bloody stucco on the walls, tapestries hanging from the smoke and the firemen's water, time passing through the footlights of an abandoned stage.

I see us again standing before Valparaiso, breathing this Chilean history, the smell of salt and tar, listening to the soft push of the sea over quiet lives in this nearly forgotten night. He is still at my side, like the head of a household who is kissing his family, his wife, his daughters, embracing his friend as neighbors do when life is pleasant and they say goodnight, sure of tomorrow.

Absorbed in thought, I try to imagine the face of Allende dead in La Moneda, and I carefully note each detail, minutely following the course of the bullets; I search for the holes and the furrows, the exploded skull and the burns and traces of gunpowder. I observe the strong robust chest, the rips in the sweater, the rolled-up pants leg, and I return to the face, that is to the head, open like a burnt torch, and then to the hands. I try to find other people there, but the figures are blurred and move slowly in the flames, with heavy rubber boots, walking from room to room, from one furnace to another, listless, full of smoke, dragging waterless hoses, searching for the lights and, suddenly, it's Tencha I see moving away in that green penumbra, walking toward the coffin in that huge space resembling a hangar; pale, breathless, frightened as she tries abruptly to lift the canvas, and then hurriedly walking through the cemetery of Santa Inés in Viña, still thinking of what she saw inside the bag stapled forever: something keeping a great silence. I return insistently to that face because I wish to understand the distant movement of uniforms in the streets and the delegation of firemen in the evening who leave La Moneda with the President slung on a stretcher, covered with a rug, carrying him to a truck with a huge white cross on its back.

Why did he go to La Moneda unhesitant, quick and hard, a submachine gun in his hand? It is possible to feel compassion, amazement and tenderness for him now. It seems he was tenaciously hunting down his enemy and hoping to find a Biblical strait gate. He fell, instead, into a trap, dreaming of wide avenues peopled by free men and women, the world before him and behind him the gray moment of deception and defeat. Some came to prowl around. Allende went straight to the outcome, without questioning his luck, a hasty and jealous guardian of his visions. Others arrived on the 11th of September to keep a dubious date with the image we had made of Chile. Allende went to meet with Allende. Later, the tortured and the forgotten, the imprisoned and the disappeared, those of us who still wander through the avenues, secretly recognize his reason. He was resolute in his search for a curtain that fell like a veil of blood, suddenly.

But let me put the future behind me. Here at Cerro Castillo, Allende plays with the zipper of his sweater and looks at me over the basket of peaches. The military aides follow the conversation very attentively and cordially, the ladies and children around the table open the starched napkins, the street urchins from Southern Chile drink their hot chocolate, Allende gets up, well-combed and stiff, greets the sailors and flies off, because all of us have lived a good and Chilean life that Sunday, and I still don't understand what it was that erased all that. Was it water on a freshly inked notebook? Or was it perhaps blood that flowed out of us and began to run down somewhere else, like when people die and don't need it anymore? What I do know is that Allende comes and goes, approaching and then leaving me, now he is here and now there, and no break appears in his conversation, truly, not even a pause or transition: we look into each other's eyes, because he knows and I know too.

I don't have his life in detail, rather some odd facts that cause me to form conflicting images of him. Who will one day be able to make a portrait of Allende? His true personality eluded the photographers. He seemed like an image escaped from a Picasso canvas, his person full of unexpected things. And these things opposed one another. He could seem smiling or concentrated, confused or convincing and alienated at the same time. They called him "Chicho," a swanky-sounding nickname. Since he cared about elegance, his enemies scornfully called him "sport." Nevertheless, at the demonstration on the 4th of September he appeared massive and serene, like a prizefighter, cautious and intent. With the people he was people. No doubt about it. What's strange is that he could play that role and many others.

I interviewed him five times, without notes or outlines, rather at improvised meetings which were frequently interrupted, breaking the rhythm of the conversation and mixing the topics. Allende resumed his monologue easily, but once interrupted he looked for new pathways; he tried to concentrate and rambled, answering imaginary questions or following associations he made on his own.

I took many photos and religiously made notes when I came home after each visit. Now I perceive that the tumultuous city, the political confrontations and contradictions, that kind of static panic and cold uneasiness that took hold of people around La Moneda, influenced what I took down. I don't have instructive dialogues, and the monologues are not always orderly. Sometimes they're just singing exercises.

I prefer to place things in juxtaposition in order to reveal from another angle the events of September. Perhaps in brief snapshots a man appears who was meeting his destiny and accepted it, convinced that in this final violent act he fully realized himself. His speeches began to come apart and the shouts were not yet heard. Allende was able to review his political history and to make commentaries or draw conclusions. Not for me, certainly, but for himself. As if he already held the "final words" microphone in his hands and was awaiting the order from the control booth to begin speaking.

When he spoke to me of his nanny, I saw in his face that she was more than simply another person. She invoked in him a very particular world, in which she seemed to grow out of all proportion.

"I had a nanny and she was fat and dark and she had many beauty marks. In her arms I slept as if in a great bronze bed. She would put me on her neck and there I would breathe the scent of trees in the summer, the odor of lakes, or the smell of toasted flour on watermelons. She lulled me and sang me to sleep through those lonely, magic years. The house grew out of the hillside. One floor on top of another, and crowned by a lookout with cornices, turrets and battlements, like a sand castle built by pastry-shaping hands. Painted wood, colored glass, a zinc roof that captured the breeze from the sky and the sea, then lost it to the rain and the wind. Yellow walls and low fences, an iridescent glass door and a huge waxed hall where pots of hydrangeas, geraniums and rubber trees seemed to float. A boy would run through the formal drawing rooms and, opening the heavy doors with their porcelain knobs, would enter a dark dining room, with a very high ceiling, loaded with red furniture and paintings open like the sea, full of fish and nets and boats. Alone, watching from the corners, as if before an altar, I measured the thickness and the depth of the sideboard, gazing at the crystal jars holding some creamy butter or a rectangle of dark quince, soft and fragrant. The lines of strangely quiet oil and vinegar in living bottles. This nanny dressed in black floated down the corridors and through the glass galleries. I would climb on her lap and fall asleep there, and sometimes we would go into the kitchen to eat raw meatballs and hide from the wind. I didn't really like her stories because they frightened me, but I would ask her for them anyway and she would sit and tell them to me, the two of us staring at the brazier, hearing doors close in the empty house and crying and screaming in the hills. She saw me grow up a mixture of boy and adolescent and part of the house. It's curious that I can't seem to clearly remember the relatives and friends of my parents. I was near-sighted from childhood, and hasty. I was always preoccupied with what others saw in me, but could not see the details in others. Over the image of my mother my nanny's image was stamped, absorbing, engrossing. My mother never lost the regulated calm and firmness of her studies in accounting. I would say that she wrote her life in a firm gothic hand. My father was just a memory, not a true presence, like my grandfather. A memory of what? Of things I would come to know later and which would hurt me. The timidity of a child is born out of certain objects that surround him and the way adults treat them. I never understood the life of my father, distant and brilliant, alien. People spoke of him with admiration but sorrow. I must have felt something was being lost: maybe his wealth or prestige or power, but I didn't know the nature of such loss, or why it was his fault that he lost it. I never comprehended the idea of a life being tossed overboard. I was impressed by his masculine beauty and enthralled by his voice and his laughter and his way of abandoning us sadly but playfully. Nanny was a warm hearth and mother was a locked door. In my sisters I saw my father's jovial spirit which they transformed into beauty and grace and a delicate intelligence.

"As I said, I had a nanny and I went to school and was known as a boy athlete, and in my house there were courtyards and trees, drawing rooms and dining rooms and a kitchen, winters and summers, wind from the sea, neighbors I've forgotten. I had lunch at Nanny's house when I was elected President because I wished to return to a childhood that, indeed, never was mine. I grew up too quickly. The years, the people, took hold of me; no one, I think, ever asked me anything—they always assumed that I had invented the answers and the memories.

"Tenderness is a word I understand, and affection. Love, since it springs from trust, is a difficult test for someone who is ambitious. One only really learns when almost everything is lost."

He was reclining on a plush sofa, ruby red, set against the east wall of the palace, between two windows that face Morandé Street, with the head and trunk leaning slightly towards the right: superior extremities slightly extended, lower extremities extended and somewhat separated. A machine gun #1651 was observed, with the muzzle and firing mechanism resting on the chair and the folding stock resting on the forearm and abdominal region.

The external police examination showed an erosive contusive star-shaped wound in the area of the chin, that corresponded to the orifice of entry of the bullet and on whose borders could be observed a discreet carbonic halo. On the right superciliar arch, another wound, which seems to be the exit orifice of a bullet or bone splinter. In the left parietal region, an exit orifice of the bullet that caused the explosion in the cranial cavity. There are fractures of the upper and lower maxillaries and fractures in the nasal and frontal areas. Lividity occurs at the corresponding level. Incipient rigidity at the level of the maxillary. Approximate time of death at the end of examination at 1800 hours was estimated to be four and one half hours, probable cause cranial encephalic traumatism due to bullet wound of a suicidal nature.

Inspector of the Homicide Brigade,
Pedro Espinoza, VEA, #1785, 9/28/73,
Santiago, Chile

I wish to understand his face that disintegrated sooner or later like the face of the young bull collapsing on his side in the slaughterhouse, some star marked on his forehead, on his woolly hair, his red wrinkles and his eyes that foresaw the blow and accepted it. Out of his memories grew a kind of nightfall or dawn, the smell of fresh blood that boils and invisibly overflows the drinking cups, passing down the streets and over the tracks, tolling the sacramental bell that goes to meet the sick. But this one falls on his back, first at six and then every half hour, rising slightly in his bed, looking at the clock and falling back endlessly, repeating what the bull repeats in the darkness of dawn moving through the pens in search of the knife he inherited in the neck, his throat filling with blood and steadying himself, in his face all the steam of long, lonely avenues, wounded, struggling to get closer to the thick wet fabric of the ponchos that cover the riderless horse standing guard, waiting for the head to fall in the iron pot set on a fire of crossed bones, sticks and stones, one lone star and one lone citizen lost and burnt in those corners where winter howls. I don't know. I said every half hour, and it must have been until two-thirty in the afternoon. I don't understand what that face hid; at that moment he must have learned to die. I only see him before me, staring at an airplane or looking at nothing, the submachine gun in his hand, measuring the emptiness of the sky, trapped in the Courtyard of the Orange Trees, through which the tanks push, on and on, without haste, Allende in the streets of Avenida Matta, no exit, no sun and no time, only the burnt hall, the rags of the slaughterhouse, the boiling brew, the ponchoed horsemen drinking, drying their mustaches, the bottle on high, and the last one, I don't know who he is, gathering up the abundant clots in his canteen for the color of the flags.

They called him Chicho, and he dressed a bit too elegantly, moving about in velvet drawing rooms and at formal dinners. From mass meetings he would go to the parks and spend twilight at fashionable Ñuñoa. He rose early and went riding along the slopes of Arrayán or the Maipo Canyon, galloping past the poplars, crossing the river, coming to rest under old willow trees. This was in the Thirties, at a time when student poets celebrated the Spanish resistance against fascism. Allende spoke at rallies in the old coliseum, down on San Diego Street. People would gather in front of *La Opinion* to await news of the siege of Madrid.

The meetings were growing larger and larger; Allende

voiced his support of the Popular Front; and, as the presidential elections drew near, the Nazis also stepped up their preparations for a coup. Alessandri, the Lion, knew how to deal with them. By doing away with the Chilean Nazis, Alessandri, unwillingly perhaps, sewed up the election for Aguirre Cerda.

Allende became Minister of Public Health He was on his way. The big time.

We are talking about a bourgeois milieu, solid middle class, with a long masonic tradition, about Chicho, descendant of a line of doctors, well-established patriarchs of Valparaiso. One hundred and sixty years of democratic tradition, said Allende, in a voice hoarse and emotional. This is the History of Chile: respect for the Armed Forces and the Constitution. Who opposes this? His advisor answers: there's a cold, fanatical man, obstinate, ambitious, aggressively proud of his pious *Falangismo,* a dubious strategist for a very compromised democracy, disciple of Maritain and Laval, supported by colorful singers crooning arias and boleros—he suddenly screams and it's his way of laughing; add a big fat old man, a bully, surrounded by rich cowboys, executives and magnates (and don't forget poker players), and by machine gunners and amateur pilots; executioners bearing long pedigrees; muggers to be touched only with a ten-foot pole; centurions of the night, called upon in moments of crisis to defend their privileges, austere financiers, conservative gymnasts; add also a wisp of an admiral, with a mustache waxed and prickly, and a voice like a rolling gun carriage; another mustache, smelling of whiskey and pipe tobacco; another crazy fellow, a man of few words, scary; finally, the greatest mustache, the cop on the beat, with nightstick in hand.

Of course there were others. They're not to be laughed at. Allende shot it out with them all. They jumped him at the pass.

Slowly, now that he's finished his short journey and I am beginning mine, I have memories of the Allende I met in New York, while I followed him in a crowd of photographers, looking (hoping?) for a snapshot of something unusual, perhaps brutal, worthy of all the front pages in the world.

He liked me from the beginning. I had long hair and a really thick beard. Nevertheless, he spoke to me as if to a little kid. He noticed my lack of militancy. Perhaps it interested him that I was learning my lesson while looking through a camera in the street, and not in books or in cell or union meetings.

He wore a camel-hair overcoat, a Russian fur cap and chamois gloves. In the big sitting room of his suite, we crowded around him and listened as he, for the first time, was making direct charges against the power behind the multinationals.

"We come unarmed, accepting the chair they denied us before, joining the round table where we listen and then begin to talk. I had heard they could invade Guatemala and Santo Domingo, invest in Nicaragua, provoke El Salvador and Honduras, go under Costa Rica and squeeze their fingers around Panama. The experts wanted to believe that they would never grossly intervene in a country such as Chile. But, how can our country stop them? Can one halt the beast by brandishing one's history, prestige and pride? Meanwhile they smooth out the plans for the coup in their luminous lairs, in their aluminum bases, their iron pentagons, their vaults full of dollars. What can I do under these circumstances? I will tell you that a small country, isolated such as ours, of little strategic importance for the megatomics, could at any moment be considered expendable. Cuba is a totally different matter, of course.

"We pose new problems. We set forth the clear and simple premise that a nation with political acumen and the desire for economic freedom can develop a socialist revolution within a democratic framework. That's why we won the presidency of Chile. But we didn't win the power. Just the government. In any case, if Chile were able to nationalize its resources, redistribute its income, incorporate marginated groups into its social life, the rest of Latin America would suddenly have another alternative. Like saying: our people need a revolution, not a 'new deal' or pseudo-alliances. This revolution can be achieved through violent means as in Cuba—where Fidel fought against a dictatorship, don't you forget it—or through legal means as we are trying to do in Chile. A convincing victory for the Popular Unity could tip the political scale against imperialism in all of Latin America. We present a powerful temptation, and, obviously, cannot be allowed to win. On the very same day that I became President, they began weaving the tangled web of intrigue to overthrow us. Our middle class was unaware of the danger hidden in every conspiracy encouraged by national and international monopolies. They lacked political education and social conscience. They were the victims of panic, a panic made to order by professionals. I haven't come to the United Nations to sound the alarm. It's too late. I come to state facts and denounce a tragedy from which only the heroic sacrifice of our people can save us. I know the great powers won't listen to me. They already know what I'm going to say. They are not afraid. Neither are we. We are taking a risk. They are making a despicable transaction on the stock market. I come with a charter for the emancipation of Chile. I don't bring promises or compromises, or nuclear protection by anyone. We are a country on the road to freedom. They are trying to stop us, but we ourselves will decide, in the last analysis, whether to keep the road open or close it for the benefit of our enemies."

But he brings more than just a charter, and there's more than just one road. He comes walking towards me through the hall of the hotel surrounded by numerous people; I shake his hand. This morning I saw him remove his gloves and strike firmly against the beast that crouched in the huge auditorium, stretching, swelling, like a pale octopus, absorbing the blows. Now, Allende goes out into the street and we walk rapidly down 5th Avenue under a drizzle turning to snow. He is unrecognized. People ask who he is and photograph him as he passes in front of the ITT building. He stops before a store, window-shopping. On each corner, in the middle of the street, in front, in back, huge secret men speak into mysterious little boxes and follow his steps on an invisible map. Vibrations come and go, sound waves rise and cross bridges, under water across high seas, entangling themselves in far away towers, until they settle and are recorded in luminous IBMS. Voices grow louder around him, there are speakers in the ground and in the air. His house is one huge microphone that broadcasts worldwide to the conference rooms of all corporations and their intelligence services. The X-rays are being filed, pins begin to mark the spots where bullets will enter, and the drizzle finally becomes snow. I look at him, his mustache wet and his hat turning white. We shake hands. I don't know what to say. The white star on his jet plane shines as if it were coming out of the sea, and the black limousines again carry him quickly in search of the beast that has remained silent during his visit, putting out its web now and beginning to snare him. Yes, he says to me, we'll have many conversations, not on a political level, but rather in this tone we are slowly learning. I'm listening to his voice long after the crowds have left and the slogans and applause have ended. He is alone, not knowing whether he must leave or insist, give himself up or let himself be pushed, be raised and laid out and covered with a Bolivian rug.

Will he have time for me? Will he have time? I asked myself then. They are snipping time away as he walks through this city. There is a man on watch behind him marking his minutes and seconds, cutting away the ground he has just passed over. There is no turning back, Mr. President, no turning back for you. Down the street he is recognized by two Chilean youths and he jokes with them, keeping his distance, while the United Nations Plenary Assembly rises and gives him an ovation and he adjusts his glasses, and Captain Araya, his Naval Aide, is standing in the background, guarding his back (he himself murdered in Santiago in 1972), and he says goodby but without sorrow, slightly impatient, "impatient" *is* the word. He steps back, unbuttons the guayabera, and leaves his glass on the table and says to me why, but why does it have to be this way?

Now we shake hands, the snow keeps falling. A while ago I saw him strong and eager, now he seems tired and apprehensive, perhaps thinking up the next political move, a new start, the bad cards he draws will get better. He has lost his peace, and I don't know whether it's a faith in himself or a feeling of being drained that gives him that fixed look, but he stands again, and we see him go up to his room, though it seems as if he has stayed behind with us. He has remained.

This brings me back to the present and back to myself. My family is four more or less displaced people. Our home came apart years ago; it came unstuck like a badly glued doll house. I am sure, my father says in one of his rare moments of loquacity, that we've acted by instinct: you boys clung to your mother; she, unable to dominate me entirely, to make me conform to her schedules and, above all, to her plan for getting old, went away mad and hurt, saying she gave everything, sacrificing herself for a person who didn't appreciate her, who deceived her and plotted her old age and ruin. On my part, I refused to run away, I stood firm in my bedroom and firm in my bank account, I didn't give an inch and took the bull by the horns. I survived precisely because I stayed by myself. I did not divorce because in my family divorce doesn't exist. She got a divorce I don't know where. You know damn well where she got it, I say. He looks at me with amazed curiosity, like someone who suddenly hears a fish speak from his aquarium. As a Protestant, she never understood the virtues of a solid Catholic home. She believes women can rebel and take off for wherever they please. She also believes she should have a career and emancipate herself—in other words, overshadow me, distinguish herself, fight and eradicate me. You kept everything, I say. You pushed us out into the world with her. She gave nothing, he answers. The farm continues to be mine and my brother's, that is, what is left of it after the invasion of Chonchol and his tribe of Communists. Your roots and your brother's are mine. Don't forget it. You learned from her and her gringos how to be hippies. Here you might learn to be a gentleman again.

His logic was, at that time, irrefutably absurd. Families come undone with time and crises, he said. It is not individuals or people who dissolve them. Your mother, because she is Lutheran, tends to think of me as worthless, selfish and hypocritical. You and your brother grow up disrespectful and become hippies.

The priests, he says, demystify the church and fill it with guitar players and half-naked dancers; then they talk about justice in the fields and on the collective farms and of Comrade Christ. All these troublemakers exalt the rabble, so Allende gets elected President, a bourgeois doctor and a Mason. The Marxists are intent on destroying the country, the family, our institutions and order. They act according to their whims and twisted intentions. If the people rebel, they don't really "rebel," they become insolent and perverted. It is criminal for them to forget their station and become agitated. The virtue of the poor, he says philosophically, was always to endure and remain silent; that is the basis of their greatness. As far as the lower middle class is concerned, if they educate themselves, improve their manners and mores, they will rise on the social ladder and win the respect of the people of order. Our country was great when everyone did his duty, maintaining discipline and respect for moral values and traditions. Nowadays, the problem is clear and there is only one solution: Allende ruined us. Why did he fail? Because he had to fail. The great majority of Chileans are conservative and despise communism. Our common man is resourceful, an individualist, and will never let himself be deprived of the opportunity to rise. Allende's government failed from ignorance and inefficiency. They got their economists from Cuba—a country, as you know, with a tropical economy, where money grows on trees, and they came here to coin and distribute money: the dance of inflation. They failed. They had to go.

It's *El Mercurio* talking. He then goes on discussing the law of supply and demand, the balance of payments, the *Mir-*

istas, and he's about to go up the Amazon to the land of the apes, but he runs out of breath and pauses; he says that he is not a politican, just an objective and fair-minded patriot.

One night after dinner he speaks out again while pacing the living room with his thumb in his vest pocket, carrying a glass full of gin he makes in the bathtub. Then my brother interrupts him. There is a brief, violent dialogue. Marcelo, from the floor where he is sitting, with his blue eyes very open, without blinking, tells him, "Father, you're a reactionary, and like all the other old reactionaries you are going to get the shit kicked out of you." Father begins to grimace without finding an answer. Marcelo takes advantage of this to tell him that, "It was not you, but the monied reactionaries who sabotaged Allende; they didn't plant their farms, they bought dollars and hid them, closed their factories and their businesses, sent their kids and the women out to raise hell in the streets, went on strike at the hospitals and the courts and, with the Supreme Court in the forefront, protected the most tightly-run terrorist movement in the world, while *El Mercurio* defended them and spoke well of the Americans who closed all sources of credit to Allende outside Chile." Father finds his voice and tells him he is a dirty Communist, the years he spent in the United States didn't help him at all, and when hell breaks loose in Santiago, if he has a pistol in his hand, he will be the first to pull the trigger and give him what's coming to him. Marcelo gets up and walks out. I don't know what to do. I'm afraid the old man might have a heart attack and I stay there for a while watching him, but it seems the gin helps him and the twitching of his face seems to lessen and he sits down. Then I leave and go to Marcelo's apartment. I find him sitting on the floor playing the guitar. I lie on his bed and spend hours thinking. Finally, Marcelo puts down the guitar and tells me: someday I'm going to have to shoot him. I don't believe him, but, on the other hand, I think that they have already shot each other. There is nothing more to do.

Yesterday something happened that sounds like a Biblical parable. I must relate it as the testimony of the only ones left to tell the story, a worker from the SUMAR factory and the lieutenant in charge.

Yes, the soldiers are coming in a dark green truck. They arrived without too much commotion. At that time, that day, all of us hanging out, rubbing our hands and some women doing the wash, but most them heating water. I would say a dead afternoon. If it's Sunday, it doesn't really matter. As I was saying, we would pitch coins and the kids played ball. Those who had radios would listen to soccer games. No one stays inside, here we live with the dogs and the kids and people talk about their problems and compare their bad luck. Nothing out of the ordinary. But that Sunday the kid warns his mother and she stays in the doorway drying her hands on her ragged apron.

The shantytown is made of mud and the shacks are wood. Some of them can't even be called shacks, but we have to call them something. Due to a lack of nails, the sticks are tied or propped up, and if they don't fly off it's because the piece of tin that serves as a roof is held down by rocks.

But this tiny child, around four or five years old, looks at me with the eyes of an old man, and as I go by I put my hand on his head. He's got wet hair and I notice his pants are torn and socks are down around his ankles. The rest of the shantytown is of no interest: their roads, the water fountain, the see-saws and swings, the silent TV set or the Chilean flag they forgot to lower. I remember the kid had bloody knees and muddy shoes. Several sweaters on, all torn.

As I was saying, the day was cloudy, a day for pisco or red wine, and it gets cold here. There's no protection from the wind and everything leaks, and so the straw mattresses get soaked, which is why the women have bladder troubles and the little kid, the carpenter's boy, wets himself. There's no heat, where would we get coal, just some dry sticks and paper, and that's why you see groups of people warming their feet. So the soldiers get off, calmly, not like other times when they came running blocking people with their rifles. They went straight to the carpenter's house, I mean, because since the 11th of September they must have searched that house twenty times, but now they do it without any big hurry. It seemed to me they weren't really interested anymore.

The woman looked at me in a different way and I couldn't meet her eyes. It wasn't anger or fear or anything. A pair of eyes like stones where I could see myself reflected as a real sonofabitch. But the kid stayed standing outside. The rest pretended not to notice, as always, cool asshole rotos. *I walked up to the door and the woman stepped aside. I don't like the bitch because I know she's a hard one. Not that it matters. I went in with the sergeant and two soldiers and we started the search. Always the same bullshit. I went outside, bored. The kid continued to stand there, a huge head and skinny legs, the same as all these fucking people, with a festering mutt next to him. I look at my watch. Plenty of time for a good search up the hill. And then back to the regiment. But it's cold and getting dark. Nothing new, said the sergeant, and the stupid bitch said, don't you get tired, how long are you going to keep this up? The sergeant turned around to slap her but I stopped him. I smoothed out my gloves and gave the order to leave. And then, I don't know why, that's the way things are, I guess, I told the kid that's it, son, we're not coming back. I saw him standing there, shivering cold, alone . . . and I put my hand on his head once more. Then he spoke to me. It was the first time he spoke, and he said you mean you already found daddy in the loft? I stared at him and the child didn't flinch. It seemed like he was smiling. I looked at the others. Stiff, scared shitless. I turned and we went back into the shack. I didn't give any orders. The sergeant was pounding the roof with his rifle. Taking his time, the sergeant said, come down, you bastard, or we'll shoot your wife. Then the sucker jumped. I stepped back. He was unarmed. I had never seen him in person, I recognized him by the pictures that were published after the* SUMAR *incident. A young guy,* skinny but strong, with a Guevara-style beard, it's a fad now. He looked around hesitantly, glanced at the woman, but ignored me. The sergeant shoved him from behind and pushed him out of the shack. Afterwards, the motherfucker stared me straight in the eye, and I said angrily, what are you waiting for, and the sergeant hurried to form the squad. They put the man against the wall of the shack and lickety-split the sergeant lifted his saber and shouted fire and the soldiers fired. The motherfucker bent over and tried to steady himself but his legs buckled under him. He fell heavily. The sergeant waited. My troops waited. The smell of gunpowder stung my nose. I got very close to him. I aimed for the back of the neck and bang! gave him the coup de grâce. I stepped backwards, there was already blood and mud on my boots. And when I was leaving I saw the kid. He hadn't moved. I didn't look at the woman. I would have liked to tell the kid something, something like, listen son, your father didn't hear you. He never knew what you said. But how can you say something like that to a kid? All his life they'll tell him. Or not.

I returned to the Alameda and retraced my steps. The center of town was an armed camp. Some planes flew over. A helicopter went back and forth at great speed firing at the roofs of the Ministries. In the Alameda the traffic of armored vehicles, jeeps and military trucks kept up. Obviously the *Carabineros* were collaborating with the military, and together they were closing a pincer movement around La Moneda. I continued to walk casually and took pictures without anyone objecting. The soldiers and the police stared straight ahead and their faces disappeared into the metal circles of their helmets. They gave the impression of a military parade of combat uniforms. But near Santa Lucía that sensation changed. Now I felt that the enveloping movement came from very far away and was opening like a steel fan, embracing streets and avenues, from Americo Vespucio, Avenida Matta, Cerrillos Station and further away, closing the arc from the Panamerican highway, a green invasion, fast and efficient, against the gray sky, artillery, tanks, bayonets, a plodding movement over wet pavement, past shut-up buildings and houses, through the silent country, barely noticing the distant shining jets, keeping time with the boring rhythm of marches on the radio, searching out the bursts of machine gun and small weapons fire, but without ever seeing anyone, just uniforms advancing, because everyone had gone and Santiago was an open city, ready to disintegrate in a cloud of adobe and plaster dust.

There were fewer and fewer people on the avenue. Standing on that greasy asphalt, I saw as in a dream people moving away from me, half-flying and half-running, ignoring me or else staring with rancor and surprise, and someone on the other side, going up the stairs of Santa Lucía raising an arm in some signal I didn't understand but which had to do with me. Heavy chains hung from the bronze gates of the National Library, and next to the thick doors I saw a group of men lying on the ground, their hands behind their heads, suspended in time under the nearby gun sights, and I felt an emptiness in the pit of my stomach and an overwhelming anguish: I began to grimace and move my hands because the automatic rifles were aiming at me and I couldn't see the soldiers' faces, the one who spoke to me had no teeth and he was very pale, and he said, give me that camera, motherfucker, and he tore out the film with long bony fingers, where do you live, give me your I.D., and I gave him my press credentials and he said nothing, the other one was poking the barrel in my ribs and I thought he looked like a peasant boy with the expression of a lost calf, but the older ones were seasoned and I heard the sound of dull kicks to the sides of those on the ground. As I spread my arms, stuck to the wall like a fly ready for an insect collection, I started to shake, then they asked me, where do you live motherfucker, and what are you fucking around here for? Get home and stay home!

Our building was now echoing with the thunder of cannon fire. They're fighting in the Plaza Baquedano, father said, and from the terrace I saw the Army trucks arriving and soldiers getting out, setting up machine gun nests, and now there was heavy fighting against the Tower of the Cubans, Argentinians and Brazilians, and they answered fire, but we couldn't see anyone, and in the gardens and sand paths not even dry leaves moved, although bullets sounded closer and suddenly there was a crash in the window above and glass began to fall, and father was standing next to the curtains in the living room, terrified, looking at me, while I knelt, continuing to take pictures through the railing of the veranda, until another bullet hit our neighbor's window and left a hole and a star of shattered glass and we all threw ourselves to the ground and I slid to the window in the kitchen.

Who was fighting? Where were the shots coming from? I couldn't see anyone even though I had a view of most of the Marcoleta and Alameda gardens. Soundless bullets, invisible explosions: I don't know if they were fighting here in the Towers or if the gunfire was coming from farther away, from the other side of the river, from the Law School, or somewhere else. But a window would shatter or a truck would go by, and several blocks away I thought I saw prone soldiers taking aim and then the ashen face, the dark eyes, the toothless grin of the sergeant, and then other bodies hitting the sidewalk with more cursing and boots kicking them like pillows.

We sat in the kitchen. My father drinking gin. The phone was ringing.

I'd been living with the old man for almost two months. I don't know if the reason he gave for not allowing the children in the apartment was genuine or just an excuse: he said that with a terrace that high it was dangerous and there could be an accident. I think he was guarding his privacy. He seldom spoke to me; and though he was with me a lot, I don't think he really lived with me. Nevertheless, today, looking back on those weeks, I realize that we were very close and that he got to know me again. As for me, I discovered he was a person, after living for years with an image of a small, well-mannered autocrat. He was a timid man, without being fearful, austere, although I at least discovered another interest. Many times I saw him with a younger woman in his car, late at night, parked in front of the building, talking. She must have had problems, maybe insoluble, because they spoke until dawn without touching. She was not a beauty, just attractive; sometimes she gave the impression of being a little older, elegant. I know they went to the coast together. I never made reference to these things, nor did he seem to notice that I knew. He was careful, then, and cautious, but by no means a prig. Obviously, he wasn't going to get married and was happy in his little corner living like an angora cat, comfortable, with a servant who came by day but with whom he had no communication.

Our dialogues were never complicated, although I now know that certain things about me worried him: he accepted my separation from Luz María; he did not understand my relations with her and the children; he must have thought I was a very vulnerable sentimentalist. He was upset by my faith, which was outside his routine and ceremonial Catholicism. He was afraid for me. He wasn't overly affectionate; on the contrary, he pretended a certain coolness and indifference. Nonetheless, I found him looking at me with pity several times, although it might simply have been affection. He liked to hear me talk about the farm and my project of buying a piece of land, but was annoyed when I spoke of a commune and of the land as a place where I was going to discover peace and establish solid relations with the workers. For him the land was an estate, the boss was boss and the peasant a slave. That is why I will never live in the country, he would say, because I was born to be a landowner and I would despise myself if I were. It was a contradiction that did not trouble him. His place was in a bankrupt society which has lost the will to fight. Others would find their ties with "Fatherland and Liberty," their combat posts in sedition, clandestine actions, club and party contacts. He would continue to be a gentleman alone, where he should be, close to the oligarchy, but without money or ambitions of power; he would remain at home, occasionally going out to his rehearsals, to his concerts, to the meetings at the club and, at night, to his mysterious release. Sundays to Mass.

Alone, face to face, we foresaw the end that would separate us. I was miserable and purposeless, drifting again; he was firmly fixed, with renewed roots in his *Mercurio* and even more confidence in the actions of Divine Providence.

He never knew what had really happened to Luz María. If he had known, he would have explained it in his own way. I had the right to her, she was still and would continue to be my wife, no matter how separated we were. But how, he didn't know. It seemed better that way. To know we love each other as we do now, risking everything on a road she chose and that I have learned to recognize, would have separated him from me forever. Perhaps he knew all this and kept silent.

The battle around the San Borja Towers was intensifying. Some time in the morning of September 11th, we saw how they took away several groups of people, men and women, in army trucks. Allende spoke for the third time that morning; we had the impression it was a farewell. When he said that we would never hear him again and mentioned his sacrifice and his devotion to the people, Father put his index finger to his temple and winked at me. Balmaceda, he said. I thought about it but I didn't agree. It is coming to an end, Father said, a few more hours and it will all be over. Everything. Absolutely everything, and he gave a little sigh and looked at his watch. The announcer said that Allende had received an ultimatum: he was being given a few minutes to surrender, otherwise La Moneda would be bombed by the Air Force. I was surprised at my own indifference. I knew that something terrible was happening, something that would profoundly change our lives, but I continued discussing the news as if I were talking about an earthquake that was already over. There was something fatal and sad in what was happening that morning, but the old man and the son were avoiding it. We were hiding in the radio and the telephone. People started calling each other and trading disturbing, contradictory tidbits. An old aunt calling, did you know they caught Faivovich and beat him to death? Where? In San Pablo. Another old lady was saying: Negra Lazo got into a truck full of cops and killed them all, with a bomb. What about her? They killed her, of course. Or the accountant would scream: Altamirano is dying, they have operated on him three times, he was trying to get out of the country with two million dollars! And the rest of them, the old man would ask. They are being shot one by one in the Stadium. That's a lie, my father would say, Altamirano is hiding. But they say that Allende is giving up and leaving on a military plane to Mendoza. We heard from a reliable source. The radio announced that at that moment Vergara and Flores had left La Moneda and were negotiating.

The shooting decreased. From time to time a machine gun burst or some distant shots. At eleven thirty in the morning everything was calm. People waving at each other from balconies and terraces. Noontime came cold, gray, and with a compact, leaden sky. Looking out at the statue of the Virgin on San Cristóbal hill, I asked myself if the end was really near. I was waiting for a miracle, really, and the more I looked at the effigy the sharper became the sensation of distance and the harder the mass of the hill, and I no longer saw the statue flying, covering us, but instead, unmoving and alien. She too was a target in this catastrophe, sentient, waiting, the same as we. Then I told my father the planes were coming, surely the beginning of the end.

I went out on the terrace and watched two jets go by. They must be measuring the distance, I said. I don't know what expression the old man had; I didn't see his face until much later. After, I remember the passes at rooftop level, the explosions, the flames crackling on the sides of the planes when they shot their rockets, the clear sensation that with each bomb a wall fell and another wall and another between that trembling old man hiding in his rat hole and me trembling out there on the terrace, hitting the deck to avoid an invisible superior fire power that was not yet directed at me.

Everything's gone to hell, I said, when the jets went out of sight. I looked straight at him and added: you're scared shitless. So are you, he answered. He smiled.

And a strange association of two people in hiding began, frowning or avoiding each other's faces, while the building spun with the shots and at each turn they lost a little without showing it. But no loss could bring them together.

My fear was not the same as my father's. In my case I was surprised to see how I did not participate in any fighting or take any decisive action. The duel seemed to involve people who suddenly learned to hate an unexpected image of themselves, while I was looking for mine without hatred, but without pride either, and I had to find it in terror. Neither one of us was going out into the streets to kill. The future, his as much as mine, was clearly written in the blood that had begun to spatter the houses, the barrios and the public buildings throughout Chile. It was now dripping over the slogans written in brush strokes on the walls and bridges and roadside rocks. And you knew the time would come when powerful hoses would wash down the squares and more modest sponges would wipe away the remaining letters. Words are taught in blood. We were told the old schoolteachers used to say that when they beat rebellious or lazy students with their rulers. Words can be learned, but they also hide as much as they reveal. Suddenly, a young father falls on his back in Plaza Constitución. He lies there with a bullet in his forehead, a puddle of blood spreading around his head, and the children he was holding by the hand kneel at his side and try to help him get up; they don't even cry because they can't comprehend what has happened. The man has an expression of uncertainty. The children look at him, tug at his arms. An ambulance goes by, slows down a few seconds, then speeds away. The image of that death is in my camera, but it doesn't tell me anything until that image and my eye coincide for the first time. When I begin to develop it in my darkroom, I am developing myself, eyelashes moist with blood, my hands trembling. The children and I are waiting for the image to come to life and begin walking again. And suddenly there are two dead, he and I, and my stupor turns into anguish and gradually shame.

I don't want to, I tell my father when he suggests I go down and stand guard with the other men. Stand guard against what, why? No one should be allowed in the building, he says, no strangers. Strangers? Enter the building? We are all strangers right now, there are no closed buildings or doors, we are all out in the open. Absurd, he says, the Towers will be defended by the Armed Forces, but first we have to get rid of the foreign terrorists, and keep them out. He then proceeds to shock me with a little speech that doesn't sound like him at all. How can you ask for peace and order, he shouts at me, if you are not willing to fight for it; if it is given to you, it won't mean a thing, since you haven't sacrificed anything or given of yourself. You will have to adapt or run away. Son, you have to be a warrior to survive these days, he declares with a sigh.

Two words bother me: "son" and "warrior". He has given me a title and wants to add another, but he asks me to first deserve it. I try to explain to him that "warrior" is not a degree given for conforming to his set of values. I want peace, but I want it to be just. I want to practice it in body and soul, I tell him, so it can be recognized by those who push me spread-eagled against the wall, pointing their guns at me. Today they live according to what they destroy. Look out there. Everybody is hiding, stepping carefully over the blood like wild animals as they take over a disintegrated city. I can't stop them from killing. They would just as soon kill you as look at you. They've taken over the Towers, you say, and they won't know what to do with them, except fill them with dead bodies. As long as they kill, they'll live.

We're going to be here for years: my father drinking his gin and answering the phone, me taking pictures through the bars on the terrace, up in the air, as if in a cage full of stray bullets, patiently building up a kind of balance. Our composure and our perspective desert us gradually, along with our hope: one listening to the shots and calculating distance and caliber, the other knowing less but feeling more, convinced the shots won't stop until they're much nearer.

And now I need to review some facts that will help me understand the reason for the commitment that finally freed me from the cage.

When Luz María went away and my mother stayed with the boys, I knew I could not be an essential part of changes in which I saw myself almost accidentally involved. To begin with, I thought I was the cause of the decisive crisis: our marriage was falling apart like a film in slow motion, a big explosion where pieces of everything, persons, objects and earth, fly through the air, a fountain of ruins where nothing can be made out; but the catastrophe has a familiar air, and then I appear, and objects and people return to their logical locations and the action acquires its natural rhythm again.

Summertime. We walk in the dusk. Everything is trembling and luminous: cars, trees, doors, streets, coming together on another level, limp and sweaty, but also fresh and green and blue. On the terraces of the apartment buildings, graceful figures dance an interminable ballet with white balls that float in the air, before they descend to blend into lamps and flowers finally sticking to the melted asphalt. There are black bushes and others violent yellow on the edge of these days. The players don't talk, wearing weak smiles and wheezing. We are lying in a park and a crowd of blacks sing and dance in long dresses and white wigs. The smell of cows rises from the ground. It's dark. A few steps away a man in shirtsleeves has taken his woman by the waist and grinds his pelvis up against her until she opens her thighs and they topple into a heap next to the dark car. Later they keep kissing on the ground. Luz María takes her hand away. She smokes a cigarette and says it is impossible for her to decide, that the problem is not whether I live with her or not, that I can't offer her Europe instead of Chile, that I shouldn't pressure her because she has to be alone once in a while, that my mother envelops and crushes her. I'd like to start all over again, but I don't know how. She says it all with a very calm voice and disarms me because there's no room for me to add a word, and every gesture of mine hangs in the air without an answer. There she is, sitting on the grass, I can hardly see her; the others are still busy on the ground, the black girls are singing, the trees never go anywhere; and nothing happens in the clear, nighttime sky. Luz María, in a T-shirt, her long neck slightly bent, her face hidden, her arms around her knees, looking, listening, making me feel like a woolly, overheated lamb, unable to move. She stops talking. Then let us leave summer alone, at night, on the vicuña rug, arched and passing out. Now that slow song and those long, bony hands say something else. We must go, then; a little crying when her face can't be seen, more things may happen, quite different things. She has made no promises. She has asked me not to call her.

But now I sense another meaning. I think it must have been obvious to her that nothing was over, that we were playing games and postponing the meeting where everything would be seriously discussed, maybe for all time. I realize that Luz María was discovering herself through me; she felt trapped or bedded down, living comfortably or uncomfortably in me, and she didn't get angry but a little sad, and that's why she didn't discuss living alone. Serious, calm, she knew it would take some time for me to get over it, but likewise she recognized that someone (who, really?—her? me?) would still recline between us, judging everything in silence, while Luz María talked about a "new life." She wasn't talking about me. At least she didn't convince me she was talking about me.

Coming back to Chile, knowing I was all alone, leaving a kind of limbo, I found it was still possible to discover an open door and be in the presence of real people. My brother had a sense of personal commitment that I didn't share. This commitment tied him to certain things that were going to happen in which he wanted to play a direct role. My obsession was to blot out a number of failures and turn them into the reason for finally creating something that might redeem me in front of those I had hurt. I wanted to mend the victims. Today I see too that some I thought were victims were fellow travelers, suffering with me because they had no one else to accompany them. Besides, it is well known that victims are made but cannot be unmade; we cannot even mop up the circles of blood; the tracks remain, blurred but painful.

I remember the many days and nights Luz María and I were joined by every member of all the bodies God gave us, unconscious and even inspired; sharing, giving, receiving and holding back; emptying ourselves with eyes closed; and I see that neither of us stopped being alone. I mean before, during and after the fainting. I must confess also that most of the time the people in bed were Luz María, myself, the children and my mother, and that the chaos, with its anguish, made me weep. When I try to imagine Luz María, I remember some gesture that perplexed me, some part of her body that hurt me, things which are finally not her, and yet I can see her naked back, the rug we trod on the way to the bathroom, her face wrinkling up, breathing heavily, and also, a comb next to the sink.

One night Luz María was leisurely dressing, and as she brushed her hair I was amazed to see her bare thighs glow and her waist brighten, and getting up I went to kiss her from behind and took her hips to turn her; then a pencil rolled off to the floor and the doorbell rang downstairs—what the hell—and the doorbell rang and rang and we paid no attention to it. All I could see were mirrors reflecting her legs spread wide and the expression I had of a stranger worried about hiding or finding something. Then I closed my eyes and forcibly slipped over her right there on the floor.

Afterwards, everything started over, me on my back watching while she put on her eyes and eyebrows and lashes and lips. The doorbell was still ringing. Tired, I got dressed and went downstairs to see who it was and what they wanted. Late now, the street lights on, the street empty, only trees and a fine early summer breeze. No one was at the door, and I walked out looking for the edge of the river, wondering why everything was out of place. I felt that we were going somewhere, that I was carrying her along pathways of sand and green leaves, setting her afloat in the lights on the river, pushing her toward the bridges where the final struggle was waiting, the one for which Luz María had prepared me. I think I left the door open. And didn't go back.

All this is so far in the past. Now I know that Luz María was aware of some details I didn't recognize. We had begun something, and she and I would help each other.

I would look for Marcelo on the BMW 500 and we would go off to take pictures. In the brilliant spring sun, the city was a wide-open field of armed men and terrified citizens. I can't forget the faces of Santiago those last days of September. A policeman pointing his submachine gun from behind a tree arrests us. Other police get off the truck. They put us against a wall and begin to search us. Marcelo says something which I can't understand. I hear the muffled sound of a kick and turn around to look. Somebody hits me in the kidneys with a gun butt. They go through our papers. I don't move, aware of the people watching from a distance. I feel nothing. Time goes by. They can't decide whether to keep us or let us go. Then suddenly, I notice some stains and holes on the wall next to my face. Now I understand what Marcelo was saying. We are standing facing death, more than one death, some screams and shadows scratching, falling violently from above, from very high up, painting an incomplete testimony in blood, filtering through the holes the bullets left in the wall. Here, yesterday, they stood up two adolescents and shot them because they took them for *Miristas* sniping at night. It was past nine and the guard cornered them on the spot where the whores wait, right in front of the movie house, the soda fountain and the pinball machines, and they decided to teach them a lesson, but the lesson was also learned by the parents and brothers of the executed, who were looking through the window and didn't dare go out or scream or protest because these things people learn in silence. Then, my brother and I put our cheeks against the wall and slowly recorded those faces, those nails, those open mouths and that death as we fiercely embraced the city that now had no limits.

They gave us back our credentials and we took off on the cycle again, stopping on Costanera close to the brewery to look at the fishermen. A paddy wagon opened its back doors and hooks and ropes came out; some people were walking on the river bank and the fishermen were going down lacing up a heavy bundle and then dragging it trying to dislodge it from the rocks where it was stuck. I put on the telephoto and brought it closer, focusing on the shape of a man, ageless, face down, swollen, dripping and full of holes. The swift current had loosened his jacket. He was snagged by his belt and jerked out of his voyage, tied securely so he couldn't run away. The operation had to be fast because other corpses were already sailing past: the flotilla of death.

Then we rode to the *Venecia* on Pío Nono and ordered a bottle of wine and sat there drinking, waiting for someone to speak. We drank slowly, knowing the BMW would demand more of us. I remember these details because when we went to my brother's apartment, I was thinking that Luz María had to be told, since she would need help as badly as we did, and those holes in the wall were hers as much as ours.

Life in Santiago demanded of people an astuteness or a courage to which they weren't accustomed. Salvation stopped being an abstract term and became an everyday task. For a person like Luz María there ought to be a calling too, but nothing epic or noisy, rather the simple revelation that if we are to survive, it will be because resistance is accepted and action is not feared or postponed.

I don't know the details of her militancy. I never asked her. Nor did she give me any indication. I suppose she and her comrades wrote slogans on the walls, perhaps helping to find refuge for the persecuted. I don't know. In reality, there is no significance in individual acts demanding greater or lesser risk. Significance resides, rather, in the resolution to confront the enemy with the means he himself has chosen. A small band of young patriots, men and women, goes throughout a clandestine land undermining the basis of the dictatorship. Another band, much more numerous, better armed, mastering infinite networks, advances implacably and bloodily, following closely the tracks of the first. One error is enough to spring the trap. The names are erased and it keeps on going. Time can be an ally, but it is also felt to be another name for that same trap. Days, weeks, months, years? How long does terror have to endure to become institutionalized and for us to convert ourselves into contemplative neighbors in a closed city? People learn to keep quiet and also to protest and resist quietly.

Luz María worked in silence and methodically. What she and her friends didn't tell was written afterwards in sensational headlines and military reports of brutal precision and verbal economy.

I don't want to create the impression that I was keeping myself behind or outside of a determined movement. The problem created by the dictatorship was handed to me in personal terms: I had a small, a very small world of loved ones in the midst of a labyrinth of violence. I had to save myself or disappear with them. A time would come when Luz María would confide in me, when my father would finally see what Marcelo and I had already discovered. When that moment came, it would find me ready. Perhaps still afraid, but now without doubts or indecision.

Luz María never argued with me. Her group considered me some kind of sad fellow traveler. They didn't understand or accept that I could take religion as a mystic trip. Luz María reacted against her own people, criticizing their naivete; but at the same time she was interested in their Christian collectivism, which could turn into outright activism. I was attracted by certain things that required moral courage, but not a simple, clear definition. I liked the idea of proving oneself to others, a kind of intimate heroism that breaks down hypocrisy, acting with conviction and strength. Among other things, Luz María's aggression against her mother fascinated me, although I couldn't understand it. It wasn't exactly a rebellion, at least not in the ordinary sense. Luz María pricked holes in the balloon of the housewifely, well-fed, militaristic matron. And I think the needle hit its mark, for she saw herself going down Costanera carrying flags, reaffirming our national machismo with self-righteous, pious acts that no one in his right mind could take seriously. The pin-pricks—words and, later, actions—were also aimed at all my relatives. She told her mother that, if she had been in Chile for the Red Rocks Festival, she would have gone to the mountains and returned very pregnant. Speaking seriously, her throat trembling, her shirt tail out, wearing blue jeans and sandals—her mother reacted rabidly against her. Or Luz María might remain silent, as if her dialogue were not the one heard by others but rather one she followed secretly and orchestrated from within. I would search for her eyes that refused to meet mine. But they let me know she was aware of my following her internal conversation.

The religious war, at that moment, had no future. There was a cellular division, if you could call it that, and the reborn uptown boys and girls came down the Alameda to the center of Santiago; some went even further and entered the slums, not like their mothers who used to disperse milk and sweaters for the babies, but rather to sit down and discuss, wash asses and distribute pills, paint signs and posters, nail boards, and seriously consider the problem of the others—relatives and friends—who came into the barrios too, with helmets, sticks, chains, and handkerchiefs over their faces, to overthrow Allende and the Communists.

I don't think Luz María's activism was what the professionals call "elitism," the revolution the kids made from forum to forum, amid typewriters, guitars and shovels. It was more intimate and less elaborate, involving the risk of physical harm. Her group, in those days (before September), was looking for the MIR, but hadn't as yet found it. In July, when I arrived, the contacts were about to be made and Luz María waited calmly. I don't think she cared about my photographic excursions on the motorcycle.

It was then that the rightist campaign against Allende was at its height: Thieme's flight, his disappearance at sea, his reappearance in Mendoza; gathering cash for the growing conspiracy; the high school students' marches near La Moneda; the old bag who stuck out her tongue at General Prats and the wives of the generals who demanded his resignation; the long lines that stretched around the city; the land seizures in the South and the incredible forums on television under the prognathic smile of Father Hasbún.

Luz María and I never talked at her house. Her mother had meetings with the ladies from Feminist Power. They collected money and food for the truckers on strike, and sometimes went and threw wheat and corn at the soldiers on guard at the Military School, while those with the loudest voices cackled at them and yelled "chicken!"

Sometimes we went to the Casa de la Luna, but we couldn't stomach all the gringos, with knapsacks and babies on their backs, who wanted to talk. We preferred to go to the UNCTAD square and watch the afternoon glow on the iron bars, from window to window, long afternoons with sudden bursts of light and tiny birds that flew from the fountain to the little tower of white stucco and shutters. Or we would go to Lastarria and search for books, or lose ourselves in the surrealistic interiors of the antique shops on Merced, asking for old pharmacy jars or a covered brazier we never found, and sometimes we would continue to Santa Lucía and climb up a little, because Luz María got a thrill kissing me among the couples of off-duty cops and maids, in the bushes where peeping toms and onanists moved softly crushing ferns, sounding like rabbits, with the drunken smell of the grass, the moist earth and the juices too, because it was almost spring.

Luz María accepted me without promises, without explanations. I had the impression that when she closed her eyes I disappeared and I wondered what I was doing alone. I could never quite find her, no matter how much I searched inside her with eyes, lips and hands; but the search had to continue and it was my true occupation, the most serious, the only one I pursued with real passion. I think she tried to make me understand that nothing tied us together, that all our meetings had to be uncertain for my own good, so that sometime I would learn to live honestly and we would each come to respect the other's irrationality.

The only thing left is to keep undressing her, I thought, and I undressed her on the little bed in Marcelo's apartment. Undressing Luz María was like watching a brook barely moving, transparent in the encouraging shadows, flickering light and dark. Her hair flowed over the sheets, beaming back the light from the mirror on the dresser. We never spoke. Sometimes she would run her fingers through my hair or sink her nails into my back, but she wouldn't open her eyes, and that obstinacy would drive me crazy as in the past, because I didn't know what she was planning, if she was truly aware that she wasn't alone, and if she would come back after leaving my arms.

As I have said, the 11th of September we telephoned each other several times. It never occured to me the line might be tapped. I would tell Luz María things that might have been dangerous if overheard by the accountant or the widow; for example, the details of the fighting around the Towers, the movement of troops and civilians.

That evening Father and I heard a broadcast from Spain. The National Radio of Lima had already announced the death of Allende. The Spaniards seemed to know the details of the fall of La Moneda that others didn't. I called Luz María and told her. She waited for me to finish relating my rumors of death, missing persons and resurrections, then told me she had to see me. Can you come out, she asked. It was impossible. Tell me, no one is listening. She told me not to be naive, she wasn't talking about going out through the main door of our building and paying respects to the military but sneaking out surreptitiously and going to an address on a street close to Pedro de Valdivia because I was needed. She told me about a woman I knew, with that way of saying things in code that one should understand and never does. I said yes. What is wrong with her? Nothing is wrong with her, Luz María said, that's just it, something might happen to her. But what is she afraid of? What can they do to her? Her apartment was searched and they found weapons. She can't go back. She's in hiding. What good was the secret if we were already talking about weapons on the phone? Can you come or not? And Marcelo? He's at the house. No he's not. We just talked over the phone a few minutes ago. Marcelo is already at the address I'm talking about. I wanted to ask if he was armed too but she hung up.

My father was listening to the radio. The shooting went on but with another rhythm, it would come closer and then recede, the explosions were from heavy weapons, somewhere on the outskirts. The accountant came while I was talking to Luz María and told us that the Air Force was beating the shit out of the industrial belts. Now they were bombing the settlements because they're infested with *Miristas*. It's all over, the old man told him, trying to get rid of him. The army is consolidating its position. Then there was a big explosion downstairs. We looked through the blinds. A thick column of black smoke was rising on Marcoleta and downstairs upside-down wheels were still spinning, a police van was burning. The explosion was followed by a lot of shooting back at the southern Tower and a pincer attack. Neighbors were turning their lights off. We closed the windows. My father was pale, sitting stiffly in his chair. He turned the radio off. The accountant had come over to tell us that the *Miristas* were being hauled to the Stadium and that he knew from a good source that Vergara was beaten to death. What seemed to delight him was that he was beaten. He said beaten and looked at us, waiting for our reactions. The old man got up and went to the kitchen to pour himself some more gin. I turned on the radio and Spain was broadcasting music. My father and I remained silent. You could hear the sound of boots and spurs on the stairs and in the halls. The old man was smoking, still scared.

And then something odd happened: through the solid door I could see marching down the corridor a rather polite army officer, vaguely insecure, and two soldiers with submachine guns; although they were walking rapidly, they didn't seem to go forward; they were coming straight to our door but they would never get there; the three of them stared directly at me and the officer recognized me and tried to tell me something with his eyes; in a deep trance I continued to observe him, making an effort to understand his secret message. My father had turned completely white and shiny in his chair. From the movement of his lips I understood he was praying. Suddenly, the vision disappeared, but I continued to hear the sound of boots and doors slamming on other floors. A sad conversation seemed to surround me. Someone moaned with tender words, as if speaking of an ancient grief, of a betrayal waiting under yellow light bulbs in tired houses with old rugs that smell of cats, huge cold bathrooms, stoves where books of memories burn. Then the voice of the viola wailed about the frustrations and rage, never begging forgiveness, but explaining, not avoiding a burning truth, but confessing it, yielding without desperation, with a long, sweet song. Then some unexpected sounds. I thought they must have been bodies that fell and never stopped falling, sliding down the walls as the lights of the Stadium blinked on. In the red night there was nobody there, in the bleachers or on the field, just the sound of the distant city like an orchestra in the air, a huge, resounding piano, some meditative strings, Luz María calling me without saying my name, just moving her lips, until the lights in the Stadium went out again as the smell of grass came back, and there we were in the foothills of La Reina looking at how the city had caught fire and the trees fell like buildings and the river dragged its corpses and Luz María was stroking my forehead, giving me strength, and we both understood that the vision had to be the death of one or the other of us and I began to discuss God. I said He did not prepare chalk circles where we could be safe. His care is not for us. It's for what we leave of ourselves in others. We have to go out and face the dangers and say goodby, glad to have loved each other, while trying our luck with God's loaded dice.

I knew the nightmare patrol was coming for me and that nothing could stop it. I knew their secret and terrible steps; the sound they, not I, would never forget. At that moment a bird began chirping out on the terrace. From the shadows a cat pounced, but the cat dashed off in pain when the bird hopped on its back and pecked for all it was worth.

My father went on praying, muttering the words, and asked me if I was going to bed or wanted a cup of tea. I said no, I wanted to hear the music till the end. The viola and piano intertwined and I asked him why the orchestra had not come in. He said yes, the elegy is over; Brahms the man was heavyset, short and bearded. He said it as he stirred the glass of gin with his finger.

The music was drawing to a close in ever-widening circles, and the park became a series of flags flying without poles, like red larks fluttering through a fire. I was filled with a sensation of power rooted in melancholy, because I knew it was those voices which hurled Luz María against me: they were letting us in on the secret. In the final chords, grandiose and mellow, the two of us foretold our separation like an absolute truth which reveals everything, a struggle and a sacrifice which would unite us always.

Later they raided the building not once but several times. Wednesday I began to go out again on the motorcycle with my brother, and we'd split up at the Law School. He was high on a sense of accomplishment, confronting the soldiers and the police with his camera while they pointed at him with their automatic weapons. In my case, I was living through a disaster I still didn't comprehend but which hung over me like an imminent collapse. There were ruins I had to gather up into images before they became ideas. I shrunk from the violence of those days and the concealed cruelty of those nights. In the morning a few bodies would be found in the middle of the block, on some roof or next to the curb, usually in places where they would be noticed. People on their way to buy bread would glance at them out of the corners of their eyes and continue on their way. These corpses were dark, covered with newspaper, shot full of holes. Marcelo and I went to the morgue and took some pictures, awful scenes fixed in a chilling instant. The relatives would show up in black, stare at the lists in terror, hand over papers, fill up their coffin and depart with tears streaming down their faces. Next to a door, standing in an absurd line—there was no need to form a line—I saw some women and got close enough to photograph them. The image turned out to be a bas-relief of shadows and eyes, night against day, figures coming out of the wall wearing dusty black, watching to see who came up to join them at the cemetery. The shutter keeps clicking and the black and the faces recur again and again, jutting cheekbones, angry looks almost forgotten after so many burials, beautiful dark women and their children groomed like pages for a savage burial on some open field.

Marcelo went to the National Stadium to take pictures through the bars and got arrested. They made him stand spread-eagled against the wall. The people waiting on the other side of the street for their relatives stared in silence. They kept him like that for almost three hours. Then he was taken into the Stadium to a room under the Presidential box where he was interrogated. He was released in the afternoon, saying he'd been well-treated, except for being slammed in the back with a gun butt as they took him in.

Luz María was waiting for me in a student hostel on Pedro de Valdivia Street. Through the blinds we would see truckloads of soldiers speeding by, always aiming, fingers crooked on triggers, looking the other way, as if they were afraid an eye contact might discharge their weapons. The patrolling jeeps would arrive, stop, and the raid would start. There wasn't anything in the house. Sometimes they rifled through the books and shoved the students against the wall, taking some away and then coming back. They weren't going to find any weapons among these blond-headed peaceniks. The woman Luz María has hiding was not here either, but the entire group was mobilized in order to help her.

All of a sudden the look of the streets changed, the shops bloomed with merchandise, the market was an explosion of fruits, vegetables, cheeses and fish; entire animals appeared where before there had only been entrails and bones. People filled their bags and baskets. In the evenings there was a festive atmosphere, yet looks of hatred and fear were exchanged, and I could see individuals standing on the streets and plazas who seemed to study me with steady animosity, weighing possibilities, without clearly indicating whether they were predators or fugitives.

The Junta issued its proclamations and televised spectacular photographs of weapons discovered in La Moneda and Tomás Moro. *El Mercurio* appeared and denounced Plan Z with thick headlines. Leftist leaders gave themselves up or sought asylum in foreign embassies. At six Chile closed its windows and doors. A clandestine evening activity would begin. Millions of voices spoke on the phone in low tones, with alarm, slowly; names were given, never addresses; it was sometimes hard to distinguish the ringing phone from the doorbell; boots and rifles echoed louder and softer; shots rang out; no voices; no screams. An airplane buzzed like a hornet over the roofs of the barrios, slow, bored; the firing of small weapons followed it and it would wander elsewhere. Not long after, shooting would break out a few blocks away and the voices would return once more to the telephone, weaving a thick net of fear, shot through at times with obscene euphoria.

Thursday morning the phone rang and Marcelo answered it. He sounded worried, looked at me, covering the mouthpiece, and said: tell them it's the wrong number, hang up. I took the phone. A relaxed voice spoke of a massacre, they needed a favor of us, too much? After hanging up I told Marcelo I didn't know what was going on. It's a trick, he answered. Everybody knows that none of them is in the Stadium. Even *El Mercurio* said so. The phone rang again. Later a jeep went by and shot out all our windows with submachine guns. We threw ourselves to the ground, but someone was able to look out and see a *Carabinero* jeep. Who called? You couldn't understand the voices on the phone anymore. What remained of the passive panic of September 11 was the memory of terror and rumors. Now the voices hid weapons and unquestionable death. The resistance had begun.

That afternoon, Luz María came to the Towers. The old man had gone out. I realized that it wasn't going to be the afternoon I expected. So much has happened in so few days! For me the horror became anguish. I'm not speaking of the dead—I didn't look for them in the streets, I carried them in my eyes and spent hours with them in the darkroom, discovering secret wounds in the red light that enveloped me like an underwater bubble. It was the cool horror of slow destruction, a ruin that tore all of us to pieces, turning us into reclusive families, pale, silent, distrustful, obsessed with a myth that was burning and smoking, while others collapsed like plaster statues; afraid of a barrio strangling the comfortable apartments of San Borja, of a cemetery invading the city. Luz María told me she was at the San Cristóbal Sheraton. She said the tourists were enraged because the bar was closed. Sit down. But I wanted to kiss her. We had to erase some of the death, that same afternoon, in a room where we weren't supposed to kiss.

Luz María kept her leather jacket on, made tea, and we sat and drank it on the floor, near the terrace. She was making me feel the distance, making a silent reply to something I hadn't yet said, paying very little attention to me. Her hair, darker now, fell over her face, and in her eyes sat a kind of annoyed curiosity, almost a plea, which I couldn't fathom. She spoke about the children.

What would become of us? I thought of the hundreds of kids I'd seen today, in their white smocks, diligently washing the walls of the Mapocho where the *rotos* had scrawled when they had a government: thought of my own kids wiping history from their books, cautious, afraid, chestnut-brown and blond, with Vitacura bulges and boutique jeans, learning quickly about the cooperatives from Old Portugal and about geopolitics from Brazil.

But my children wouldn't leave and neither would I. They can't erase us like some old slogan on the Chilean walls. Everybody insists that children go out and coat the past with white paint, but it can't be done, I said, and we're staying. I'm going to do a film. Marcelo will publish his book of photographs abroad or underground. What I can't figure out, she said, is you riding around to the scene of the crime. If what happened was an earthquake, there is always something to be done for the victims, but in a few months everything will be forgotten, just some holes in crumbling walls and shacks in the mud. What have the poor people got to complain about? They have always lived that way, learning to adapt to the wall that fell on them, living out their existence or toughening up or going to pieces while they wait. All those people like your father and the fools who hang out the flag really believe that nothing has happened, that *El Siglo* closed down and *El Mercurio* opened up and that the truckers won their strike because the country believed in them. But they don't know that armed men, military and civilian, planned the massacre and are going to see it through to the end.

Curfew was approaching. The cars were racing uptown. The usual blue smoke rose from the pavement and the horns honked the same and people raised their arms anxiously at the bus stops, but the noise of the city was different, because from the mountains, El Bosque and Cerrillos, and from the small airports in the central valley, a muffled, roaring thunder was growing; the rattling of chains, the grinding noise of powerful motors, pincers that squeezed the city by the waist, tightening until it was unbearable, a hangman's noose fashioned by the arrogant cowboys from the South, tramping after foreign footsteps in the mud on a historic road littered with bodies of dead workers. Santiago, blue at noon and red at sunset, hazy and lost, no longer breathed between the ramparts of ice that were now useless to us, because they enclosed us like the walls of a strange skyscraper-freezer where bodies and shadows continued to fall.

I could imagine my two boys on that hostile evening in which the hunters and the hunted intermingled, waiting for buses, waiting for planes, waiting for bullets, and not yet seeing the man next to them, his head pressed to the window, silently crying. Now I understand my own churning sadness, those tears I shed in advance because everything was falling apart and friends and relatives went in and out of the morgue the way we once strolled through the patios of La Moneda; and I told Luz María I didn't want to leave either, although the people who blew up a truck full of policemen scared me as much as those who bombed a barrio. Luz María said she wasn't talking about being militant. To follow Christ was to follow the people, the poor who had no embassy to hide in tonight, no farm to cool off on, not even an apartment to hole up in or an airplane to fly them away. They'll be standing in line once again, mourning for the bag of bones that fell in the river or fell in a hole, resisting, until someone remembers them like Allende remembered them and joins their fight.

I didn't say anything. What could I say? But I knew that night I wouldn't wait for the old man; I wasn't going to stand guard with those jerks at the door. I would go off with her to look for a solution to her friend the councilwoman's problem, and then maybe we could sleep in peace.

Saving lives between curfew and curfew, leading the fugitives Indian-file through the alleys of the barrio, through attics and corridors, through empty movie theaters and closed malls, on motorcycles, in cars, trucks, dumping them on bare ground, on soccer fields, schoolyards, hills and cemeteries, to save the condemned before they fell on their backs or got shot trying to escape, to take people from family closets and bury them in underground hospitals, phony walls, double floors: this was the future, and the city of those who escaped turned into a second movable city throughout the country. A whole nation was escaping and another one was chasing it, shooting at close range. Listen carefully and you'll hear the running dialogue between the blindfolded and the executioners, feel the electric shock raised to the testicles and vaginas, the alternating current between the Brazilians and the CIA, the broken fingers and backs. The country is a victim of hit-and-run in the dark, a bleeding face to the pavement.

I had been over the routes on a motorcycle, memorizing the roads that led to the morgue, but didn't understand clearly why I was doing so. I was a zoom lens slowly moving up and down, from side to side, telescoping through the night which other citizens heard but never saw, like that droning plane which also observed and broadcasted and activated the death patrols.

They never made me feel I was a part of a combat ring, but I felt that next to me, in an invisible sidecar, I carried along a warrior who would save someone's life and give someone else a little more room to breathe in and fight.

I've said I stood guard at the Tower where I lived. The great majority of the tenants sympathized with the Junta and wanted to protect our immunity. Unofficial, but already known to the soldiers and policemen of the area, the night watch was organized by a woman, an old widow, who lived alone on the first floor and studied all the neighbors' movements. She kept her windows hermetically sealed and her door bolted with four chains and locks. When you came out of the elevator you felt her watching you through a little peephole in her door. She never spoke to me or even said hello, but she stared at me that morning when I went to Recoleta. She got along with my father, who promised her I would stand guard too. Our mission was to identify those who entered the building after curfew. There was nothing to do during those lonely hours and the shooting was pretty far off, so we would open the gates and the soldiers who patrolled Marcoleta would come in and the widow would hand out Nescafé and cigarettes. The soldiers told us about the atrocities of the MIR. They acted like an army on the defensive. But they felt bound to us by a neighborly spirit. We will defend ourselves together, they seemed to say. But they never actually said it.

In the student hostel the telephone conversations were impossible to understand. We talked in the dark at night. I was relaxed as I accepted the chores for the next day's motorcycle excursions. Everyone there took risks boldly, but they also took precautions. On nights when the soldiers came I was amazed to see their indifference when they answered and showed their papers. Once, the officer took a girl out to the entrance and spoke with her. I had a feeling of a large dragnet. Danger. The few Americans all looked the same, clean-cut with glasses and hairless faces; they could be Peace Corps, Council of Churches, priests, nuns or CIA. They were in no real danger. None of them ever went to the consulate where it was well-known that no one could stand them.

The real net was closing somewhere else. Luz María came by to get me one day and we drove to the Mapocho area in her red Austin. We discussed the children. I would have liked it if she had brought them with her. It was a spring day and people were discarding their overcoats; girls with sweaters over their shoulders looked at us, smiling. I asked her to stop at the central market. We parked next to the Carmelite church and walked through the warehouses between the fruit and vegetable stands. The smell of baskets and muddy water, the fragrance of oranges and apples, brought back memories of childhood and adolescence: the sound of the bells for 11:00 Mass, the aroma of pastries and turnovers; the girl friend in Bellavista, when we used to kiss in a neighborhood matinee and feel each other like the blind; or going through Forestal Park at dusk, smelling branches and herbs from the country, proletarian water from the river, walking by scarred park benches and couples entwined in the dark and we being embarrassed, not looking; and the girls and boys who went back and forth in front of the School of Fine Arts, excited, shining, full of words that got lost among the trees; and in the bushes precocious kids undressing a little and sick bums studying them.

The sun was falling on the pines and quarries of San Cristóbal hill when we arrived at a house near Perú Avenue. Luz María stopped, locked the car and went in through the garden without ringing the bell. I followed her and we passed through a glass door into a living room where a bald gentleman opened a window, and we saw children playing, a group of young people examining the Mini Austin, an old woman, in black, leaning on her windowsill, the coppery light of dusk stretching over the low tiled roofs, some smoke and trees. I felt, as I always do in those houses, the melancholy enclosure of the patio, an air of tender hopelessness. The milk was bubbling over and spilling into the fire. We were like seated ghosts, drinking tea, eating ham and avocados, hovering around the cake as Sunday was coming to an end, the day letting go of its last light, the street and the little houses against the green sky and now blue and afterwards black and starry, and the voices of the children still playing, but duller and farther away, and the small gang on the street corner whispering and smoking, the whole neighborhood closing the curtains of summer, invisible, soft, without a future.

I was paying attention after the tea and I understood why we were there. The young comrade who spoke in a tense, sing-song voice, a Communist city-councilwoman from a tough neighborhood in the industrial zone, was now harbored in a nearby building where not only her days but her hours were numbered, and she had to find asylum in an embassy. A white-haired man was negotiating with representatives of a European country. She called him Father, and he called her by her first name. The rest listened. When the moment came, Luz María said that if the priest wasn't successful, she would make another proposal, that we could still try something else. The rest said okay. It wasn't long till the curfew, so we said goodby, thanking the lady for the piece of cake she gave us wrapped in a paper napkin. I shook the young woman's hand and saw the tired eyes looking at me with a kind of quiet confidence from behind her sleeping child.

I thought to myself, how could this young woman be in danger, who could be afraid of her or hate her, why did she hide, and I wondered if there was any place in the world for her to be what she once was. Luz María didn't say anything. She took me back to the Towers. It was before six. The old man is in Viña, I said. She didn't answer but locked the car and entered the building ahead of me. The janitor took the chains off the iron gates. The widow must have been taking notes through the peephole. We got on the elevator. I held Luz María by the waist. We went into the apartment and she told me not to turn on the lights. She opened the windows of the terrace and we saw the violet glow on the mountains and felt the drowsy murmur that rose from the park among the trees; we didn't see, or didn't want to see, soldiers and patrols, only the usual flame, the spring traffic, the small lights, the small people.

The first attempt to save the councilwoman failed. I was witness to part of the mishap. Luz María and I were riding toward Mapocho. It was midday and men and women were returning from the market without much awareness of the military trucks roaring by on unknown missions. On the shortwave radio we were listening to news of violent internal battles between loyalists and insurgent troops. A Lima station described an incident in El Bosque, officers shot in cold blood for refusing to participate in the coup, and a station in Mendoza spoke of students in the Police School in suicidal combat against insurgent units. Telephone rumors mysteriously referred to bombings of working-class neighborhoods. But now the buses went by with passengers hanging off the doors as usual, carts loaded with boxes and bags, the Santiago traffic, bored or dissembling in front of the muzzles that were not aimed at anything.

We passed the house once. We recognized the priest's pickup truck. We went on, and entering Perú Avenue we drove up to the cable car entrance and turned back. Luz María decided to buy some cigarettes. We stopped at a newspaper stand. I felt someone's eyes on my back. We had parked near the hydroelectric plant, and when we returned to the car I saw some guards aiming at us. We left without hurrying. Before arriving at the house Luz María turned and went down a street I wasn't familiar with. She stopped, lit a cigarette, and we waited for a while. If the priest can't get out, she said, we'll go through here, and she showed me the door of something that could have been a factory, shop, garage or anything else. It was one o'clock. We left the car and walked and saw, in the distance, that the priest's pickup had left. We continued walking and, since we didn't see any patrols, we decided to ring the doorbell and ask what had happened. The young man opened the door. He was not smiling anymore. The lady appeared. She looked at us with alarm and said: they took away the Father. And the girl? Luz María asked. No, she wasn't here, last night her comrades came, they had found a place for her. Last night? They took her at night? Could they have taken her to an embassy? I don't know. And the Father? He must be in the Stadium. The soldiers patrolled all night and that light plane flew over, and also a helicopter. And they found the GAP soldier! The one who brought the car and hid it in the garage. They searched the whole neighborhood. And the Father? He was here when they came the second time. Shit, he didn't have his papers on him or anything, no I.D. or even a driver's license. He gave them the address of the parish and the telephone number. The Lieutenant called and whoever answered said that the Father was saying Mass and couldn't be interrupted. Those instructions were left by the Father himself. What a hell of a mess! Well. They'll release him. I don't know. The old lady said: my husband went to the Stadium.

What's strange is to be able to say the days went by; that is, the nightmare seemed to end, but nevertheless no one went back to the old routine. The order during the day seemed genuine enough, but if one looked closely one noticed something unreal and desperate in the people who walked around downtown, in the parked cars on the corners, in stores and markets. Life went on, as they say, but it went nowhere. Who worked? Who went to the office? Who went to school? Who traveled? The fascists and their families constituted a smiling Chile, you could say euphoric and even hilarious. They disappeared to enjoy their triumph. It was the obvious thing to do. "Fatherland and Liberty" was dissolved. The leaders stopped being leaders and became government, with small letters, not on the first page of *El Mercurio*, not even on the last page. They were the government where it really mattered: in the economic administration of the country and in the secret police. The more intelligent behaved with taste and celebrated in the sacred warmth of their bedrooms. Discretion and sobriety, when one holds the reins, are more useful than vengeance. This vengeance was for unstable persons, with weak principles or none, the citizenry who found their faith once more, but not in the churches or in the stadiums, rather in the televised dissemination of the brutal repression and the constant death penalty. We have seen solid citizens laugh at the evidence of torture and ask that more of their neighbors be killed. Every day found added informers turning in more names. You could say that the country needed to let go, soothe its nerves, suddenly torture itself to find the calm that would permit it to swallow the smoke of the insurgents and the crematory ovens.

And thus life goes on, going on as a subterfuge, to keep from declaring that life really went on at night, in prisons, barracks, forts, military academies, Antarctic wastelands, deserts, in hideaways maybe, or maybe even in public, in plain sight, because how are you going to hide from that death bearing your name? This deserves an explanation. Embassies filled up and you had to get a safe-conduct pass to fly out of the country. The *Allendistas* lost their jobs and their Conservative and Christian Democratic relatives had to support them. Afterwards the Christian Democrats also lost their jobs, and this turned out to be an excessive load for the Conservatives. This was about the time they built the big detention centers, where life is nothing but a pot of beans and noodles and a wooden spoon. I never heard any more about the Father who disappeared from San Cristóbal; the Communist and her child I found out about the second week of October.

Meanwhile, Luz María and I had made some decisions. Marcelo would remain in Chile, he was planning to work with me on a photographic book about the battle of Santiago. Luz María was in touch with other groups now, and I was looking for young filmmakers to collaborate on a film about the 11th of September.

My father stopped worrying. He wasn't overcome by his bitter victory. He thought the crisis was over, the Armed Forces would give back the government to the civilians and return to their barracks, what had happened was well worth the new freedom. He would say it flatly, without even looking at the street, ignoring the stories that flowed through the phone. What is over is over, we return to page one. One day he saw a photograph of old Jorge Alessandri—immense, macabre, with an overcoat that dragged the ground, scarf, hat and cane—standing in front of La Moneda, as if he had climbed down from a monument to observe the destruction caused by the rockets and the fire. My father said something about Toesca and the Red Room, named a friend of his, a history professor, who might be able to direct the reconstruction and turned the page. But he also went to look and saw the melted balconies, the burnt beams, the stairs and corridors cut in mid-air, the plaster presidents on the floor, and then he commented that La Moneda would never be the same again, that with it a chapter of history was over, and that reconstruction was not possible because countries are not made of adobe and brick anymore, with walls three feet thick, or patios of orange trees where nursemaids can take the children to play. The UNCTAD building is suitable for the new government, he said, Chile is a country without ruins or relics, the future demands glass and steel and height.

I kept on living with him, and I can't say I tolerated him because I really didn't listen to him or care what he said. I would have been offended if he had celebrated, like the accountant or the widow downstairs or the inhabitants of the ocean liner across the street, who went out on the terrace with a flag and spoke of replacing the condor and the reindeer of the Chilean coat of arms with the symbol of a pot-beating woman.

To see Luz María in the evening, take the children out Sundays, and roam through the city on my motorcycle, was for me a way of being and not being in Chile. I had broken through the invisible circle and could not worry about what my life was going to be for many years to come: reconstruct within me the world they had destroyed, start off once more on the life I had come back to begin in my country. I knew that my coming home was part of an intention (never before stated in words) to take care of past failures in Chile and place my years in the ebb and flow I had always foreseen. What was shaping up in my country, in every contradictory way, coincided with an irresistible need to balance my own accounts, examine my roots (and I don't mean thinking about them, because with "reason" I would only hatch schemes, banalities and clever lies) and cut them or re-orient them, to discover what my incessant flight and sentimental juggling had done to me and decide what was worth saving.

In Chile the civil war that might have violently purged people like me never happened. There was, of course, an indispensable number of deaths, and a sufficient part of the Chilean religion vanished in order to make it possible to discuss some kind of future. But the devastation that went too far and the deaths that slipped down the trap door surprised the planners; these were like the hurricane that mysteriously follows the earthquake, the wind created by the fury in its own wake, which takes many days to subside. We ended up, then, frustrated by an intimate, personal civil war rabidly declaring itself inside us, while we continued to walk, pretending we were obedient and peace-loving, on the way to work—to the office, to the factory, to the barracks and the prisons. They hadn't counted on the dark terrified faces on La Paz Avenue in front of the morgue or the *rotos* who left the Stadium to get back and fight, or the silence of the spectators and neighbors in their homes or the grimacing laughter of death working overtime.

People like me who lived off images, off visions, were suddenly asked to consider the word "conscience." And I reacted sadly but forcefully. Conscience meant heartbreak, being uprooted again, fear of a new void, but it also meant maturing, ripening. Since they shook our tree and we fell to ready soil, we would make our weight felt and also the strength and persistence of our secret need.

We decided, then, to fight.

One morning Luz María called to tell me something that again sounded like code. I asked a few questions. I was determined to follow instructions exactly. I was with Marcelo that afternoon and we played a colorless game of chess, as if we were both thinking of something else. We fed on rumors. Friendships disappeared. Some left, others hid. No one made an effort to find out where anyone was. Relatives went to search through the military and police lists. To ask was to call attention to someone.

The week before, Neruda died his vast death, a death that shook the whole city from top to bottom, like those poems of his about the sea that rises over the world and falls with a huge explosion of water, salt and foam. In the papers a photograph of the cortege appeared with my brother walking, a camera around his neck, smiling. This photograph of Marcelo upset everyone. There was something sensational and showy in that foreground picture. My brother wouldn't listen to our warnings, he continued to photograph the endless funeral march on La Paz Avenue, the burgeoning parade of names, denounced, accused, condemned, missing.

Before long our motocycle will be recognized; a free, fast lens that zips alone through the streets of the city, capturing moments of repression and combat.

At precisely four in the afternoon I was supposed to stand in front of a house. As I said, I never asked for the reason, but I understood the determination in Luz María's voice. Not a minute before or after.

I maneuvered my BMW around the heavy traffic. From a distance I saw a couple of soldiers and a policeman not far from the house. I knew the street well and didn't slow down when I passed the corner. The trees were bending with a sudden wind. The park next to the large apartment building was empty, golden and dark in the shadow of the windows loaded with dry vines. I recognized the number and stopped in front of an old house, a concrete crate with the blinds closed and the entrance cut off from the street by bronze fences. The building next door was an embassy. I left the motor running. The soldiers and the cop stared at me. I leaned down toward the sidewalk as if I were examining the rear wheel. Then the door of the house at the end of the front lawn opened and Luz María appeared, and simultaneously several people began to jump the wall towards the embassy. The Communist councilwoman was among them. I saw her being lifted and then she disappeared behind the wall. Everything was over in a flash. From the street neither the soldiers nor the policeman caught the action on the side porch of the house. Luz María closed the gate, approached me serenely, kissed me on the mouth and climbed on the rear seat slipping her arms around my waist. I revved the engine and we took off.

Something told me the situation behind us had changed. I felt a chill on the back of my neck. Luz María held onto me violently. We went through the intersection running the red light. Later—how much later?—I heard shots. At whom? From whom? We were really moving. I turned and headed for Providencia full speed. Out of breath, shaking, I continued to dodge traffic towards downtown. We went to Plaza Baquedano and passed Forestal Park and ended up in a little side street next to some rather Cubist buildings, stowed away between shops and garages, coming apart and sticking together like a cluttered, multicolored collage of loose-boarded floors and glass-strewn corridors. We went up. There was a group on the third floor. Someone was playing the guitar. The smoke reminded me of the summer nights in the park when the pedestrians slow down, the birds are still and from the dry grass the fragrance of another grass rises, still drier and more golden, full of dreams and heroic acts. Luz María was calm and I began to relax a little. Someone passed me a joint and I took a hit, like someone drowning who comes up for air, and then I sank back, also like a drowning man, and the posters began to grow and come nearer and the expressions on the faces were friendly and they were marching about spring again.

It was getting dark and I was absorbed watching the Santiago dusk, slow, wide, familiar, like a subtle prairie fire, populated by bells and horns, announcing an anxiously dreaded meeting, the re-establishment of old friendship between relatives who wear coats and ties. The leafy trees leaned toward the darkest suburbs, less populated and with a smell of factories and lumberyards. My father, pale and alone, dressed in black, was playing the viola among the trees.

Luz María reclined at my side. Cold air came in through the broken windows. And also the smell of dinner, of toasted bread, of brushes and paints. Night was falling. The hour of curfew had passed. They will search your house, they will search mine. They don't come here anymore, they took away all the Brazilians and the Bolivians and the Argentines. Who's left? Who's still here? Why do you ask? Why do you want to know? Where do you live? No. It doesn't matter. Here. I'm burning my fingers. The sweet herb was now a flower, a Sacred Heart between my fingers, red and burning, a slender star of commitment that I put to my lips and kissed and inhaled with an aroused curiosity.

Did we know what really happened? The little sister jumped over the wall. Jump, sweet comrade, the voice of Atahualpa Yupanqui seemed to say, his guitar speaking tenderly, jump on the side of the good and the just, fly away with the cold and cloudless dawn because your night is almost over and day is breaking, and in my arms I lulled Luz María and her soft hair covered my eyes, my mouth, my chest, and the little star went on glowing on our lips.

I think about the word "terror." I compare it to this spring which has suddenly erupted in branches of lights, in foggy mornings and in parasols of almond and peach, cherry and plum trees. I consider this sky I know so well, comparing it to the roofs on fire during the battles of September. What's left for me? A modest grief which I drown little by little, day by day, so that I can believe that spring has also come from me and flies out of my hands seeking those people who look at me in surprise, recognize me, and as my motorcycle goes by, start saying goodby to me.

When a city climbs on another city (do you remember, Luz María?—it was an innocent guessing game), and another city climbs over this city, until man, completely lost, stops thinking and attacks with iron bars and sticks, the city of God is the first to fall, the barbarians come in, the looting begins and the great tower collapses on its bed of stones. God and worthy people will remain to make a monument out of those stones, and over that monument they will raise another and another, and once again we will have history, perhaps not the same as we had before, it won't be made of stone and time, maybe, nor of leather and steel, but it will have men and women at the bottom, lying at its base, and maybe the motionless, tranquil dead will make it last.

I came to meet myself on a corner named Chile. I have been waiting some few months. Now, only now, do I truly see the other who comes to the meeting, slowly approaching, a little faceless, but it's my step, my loneliness and my hope, and he carries this notebook I must finish now, because the city, after curfew, demands more flames, more fire, much more conscience, a lot less and a lot more life.

Now the narrator must speak, taking the time that Cristián wasn't to have. Neither Allende or Neruda had it, nor Jara, nor Olivares, nor Toha, nor Prats nor Bachelet, names that fly past like pages of a calendar on the gray screen of a silent movie. A calm narrator, without regrets, sitting on a champagne-colored leather sofa, protected by a white wall from the bullet that insists on looking for him and, up till now, hasn't found him. He looks at me, and I discover behind his glasses firm eyes that don't seem to know any of my nervousness. I can't understand what the basis of that strength is—if it's a result of militancy, of faith or obsession, or simply a whim to test my grief. But he also smiles. This man knows a lot, and what he says acts as a lid for his secrets. Besides, one day he'll dress like a civilian, another he'll wear the white embroidered chasuble of the celebrant, and others—like today—he's in the uniform of a military chaplain. He might be a neighbor, priest or warrior, or some unfathomable thing I will never discover. I say this because he had my destiny in his hands and let me go for reasons he never explained—although "let go" could refer to the strings God lengthens, shortens, seems to tangle but doesn't, which, in truth, He never lets go.

We are, then, in his office, a huge room in an ancient house, high ceiling, dark worn table, glass bookcases. He has set a bottle of pisco between us and we sip slowly. The door is shut, and outside, through the galleries that surround the garden, you hear only the paws and nails of the dog that keeps watch in the darkness. There are no other noises here. Another city separates us from the city: God's city, built around the patios, and a cemetery under a brick belfry.

I will try to transcribe his words faithfully.

"It wasn't, as you know, the first time a patrol came to the door of Cristián's building. That morning the doorbell rang incessantly and the janitor got up and opened the door for the officer and his escort. According to Mr. Montealegre, he heard the knock on his door a little after five. He opened the door himself and the officer came in. He said he was looking for Cristián. He was very polite and spoke amiably while Cristián was dressing. He looked at the photographs in the living room and asked who the children were. He said he had a son Cristián's age. When Cristián appeared they left without explanation. Montealegre says he took two things for granted: first, that the officer knew who he was, that is, knew his political position, National Conservative party, moderate but firm backer of the Junta; second, that Cristián was being taken to be interrogated about the activities of Luz María and her friends. He surmised that he would be held for a few hours and then released. He also thought the weather was getting better and that a sunny day outdoors never hurt anyone. He went back to bed and didn't get up until his other son, Marcelo, came to the apartment around 11:00 in the morning. They talked about what happened and Marcelo said he had already been to the doors of the Ministry of Defense to check the lists and Cristián was not on them. That afternoon—we are talking about the 14th of October—Luz María came to the apartment with the two children. They had tea, went over the names of influential friends who might help Cristián and then Luz María and the children left. The next day Marcelo came back and said that Cristián's name was definitely not listed at the Ministry of Defense, and that he hadn't been able to get near the Bureau of Investigation. That afternoon, Cristián's father began telephoning friends. Meanwhile, the janitor said he had seen Christián leaving the building with the soldiers and several other people (he didn't remember how many), among them a student named Salas and a woman; they had been loaded into a truck, he added, which went off down Marcoleta. On the third day there was still no news. Now the three of them, Montealegre, his son Marcelo and Luz María, went around town inquiring at police stations and hospitals. Cristián had disappeared without a trace. That night, Montealegre received a telephone call from a doctor friend of his. The message was cryptic. He said that a colleague had been at the morgue and recognized Salas there. He suggested Montealegre go to the morgue the next morning. Montealegre went alone. He arrived at the building on La Paz Avenue, they brought him into an office where a clerk took down all the facts, then opened a door into a corridor, and from there into another one, where he saw a number of bodies lined up on the floor. He walked slowly down the corridors. He says he saw about a hundred corpses and there, among the last, he found the body of Cristián. He knelt down beside him, moving the other bodies aside, and saw that Cristián had a hole in his forehead, no doubt from the bullet that finished him off."

She stared at me blankly. I suppose it was to determine the effect of her tale. And I thought, at that moment, that Cristián had not accurately described this person in his notebook, seeing her through the spying peephole, that is, according to his imagination and disgust, and not according to reality. Of course, she wasn't an old bitch; neither her mouth nor her eyes were secretive or hard. On the contrary, I noticed a certain unconcerned calm, a comfortable softness in the full bust, the fleshy nose, the maternal hands and arms. She had put down the cup and was asking me if I wanted more tea. No thanks, I'm fine. And while she continued her story I examined what her life was, what made up her walls, her shelves and tables and little packages in the kitchen. The apartment was presided over by a color portrait of a military officer in parade uniform. I've never been able to distinguish rank, but I supposed, by the mustache, the size of the cap and his look, he must have been a colonel or a commander. Maybe more. He must have died many years ago—that was obvious by the cream color of his jacket, which must once have been white, and the runny colors of the nose and lips. On another wall there was a portrait of a woman. Maybe it was she in another life. A woman with short wavy hair over her forehead and a small mouth. The figurines on the tables, the small television set, some plants, indicated an indoor life, but not a sad one, the life of an indoor apartment, without a view, except the window in the kitchen which faced a blank garage wall, and, as we have said, the peephole which dominated the entrance, the hall and the elevators.

"They came at five in the morning and the janitor let them in. There was a captain and three soldiers. First they went up to the 12th floor. They were looking for Cristián Montealegre, and they brought him down in the same elevator in which they brought Garretón and the student Salas. The Argentine couple was already downstairs, waiting to be put on the truck. The Argentine woman looked about four months pregnant, I'd say, because you can tell, don't you think? and her husband had already been detained once in the Stadium."

"But that makes only five."

"Six. I haven't mentioned Saá."

"Saá?"

"Yes, he's a young man around 25 or 26. But the problem was with Salas, who had taken sleeping pills and they couldn't wake him up. He couldn't even dress himself. That boy was very depressed all the time. He was always a little ... well, you know. Señor Garretón's case is hard to fathom; I don't mean to criticize the Junta, because you know they did their duty when it was necessary to save the country from Marxism and that lunatic we had in La Moneda—times of peace demand inconceivable sacrifices. But it so happens that Señor Garretón has a son in the army—I mean he did—and never had anything to do with politics. That he got shot is a little strange, don't you think?"

I wasn't saying a word. The gloom of the library was closing in on me, like a silence that goes from one wall to another, ricocheting until the ears buzz. The window that looked out on the garden was closed, but even so a damp draft crept in smelling of lemon and mint. I drank a tiny glass of pisco in one draught. Watched it fill up again.

"I get the impression they were killed that morning, although the bodies weren't found until the 17th of October in the Lo Prado tunnel."

Perhaps he saw my disbelief or wondered himself, because he took off his glasses, stared at me with his glistening eyes, and added:

"They may have been shot somewhere else and then taken to the tunnel. It's not easy to say, there are details missing—mass executions are always a kind of puzzle with some of the pieces lost. Probably the most important ones are lost on purpose."

The silence of that big old house was oppressing me; I couldn't think straight. The narrator played with a paper knife. He'd obviously lost interest in the monologue; it was wearing him out, and what wore him out the most was keeping certain secrets in the bulging chest he tried to soothe with Alka-Seltzer and later, much later, with milk. I didn't say that that day he covered his chest with an orange cloth. The armband and cloth changed colors following confidential instructions, some kind of password so people could tell the difference between the Armed Forces and the MIR in disguise. The khaki uniform fit badly; there seemed to be too many straps and buttons. Actually, he was just a pious person whose garments were not a vestment, wearing wrinkled, floating hand-me-downs.

Sir, I haven't denounced anyone," she said. "Military Intelligence must have had its reasons which you or I will never know, but they imposed the death penalty and so there must have been strong reasons."

Why was she on the defensive? What did she expect me to do? Denounce her? To whom? The family? What could they do to her? Cristián's father didn't blame the Junta. He didn't even think they had made a mistake. He said the guilty officer was from the Popular Unity and that Cristián was a victim of Red vengeance. No one dared ask him, when they saw the terrified look on his face, whether the pregnant young Argentine was also a subject of "Red vengeance."

"I had nothing to do with it and it's not my fault if people leave the building. Would you like another cup of tea? Forty families moved out after the executions. Are you aware of that?"

He was leaning back now, almost whispering, studying the effect of his own disclosures.

About that time I noticed he had a skull on his glass bookcase. He also kept his bottles there. When he saw me counting the teeth or the glasses or the books he smiled.

"The boys were impatient. They wanted to go out on patrol. There weren't any orders. We gathered a few things together so they wouldn't get bored. The neighbors donated dominoes, cards and checkers, but they weren't satisfied. They'd acquired a taste for action."

I could imagine the number of deaths he had seen, dressed like a soldier or a civilian or a priest. Father, I asked him, have you enjoyed the hot odor of blood? You? But I was voiceless and he never answered. His obligations began early in the morning and ended at eight at night. He sacrificed the lamb in the first rays of dawn, in a pale blue glow, with stars in the palm trees. He sipped the blood of the holy lamb, wiped his lips and washed his hands. Washed his hands? I'll never know. He helped people die.

"That skull is plastic. Pour yourself another drink."

One knee on the ground, shaking, gasping for air, choking on the smell of death, trapped in that hallway that wasn't designed for piles of bodies, my pants stained with blood or grease, I thought that body was my son, with his blank, white face, his bloody mouth, one eye half-open, the other swollen shut, blue—this was the face I loved more than anything else, which I should have kissed so many times and didn't because I was shy or embarrassed, and I choked on my tears, his name was screaming inside of me, I was lying down too, crawling in next to the corpses, searching for his head in horror as I kissed him next to the bullet hole and touched his curly hair, his filthy beard which was suddenly thin and gray, as if he'd become an old man after death, and it was Cristián. He answered with a hardness made of many years, his and mine, petrified, stuck to the mosaic with the tremendous weight of a death that bears infinitely more bodies inside. They had to drag me out. I didn't see any other wounds. Just the hole in the forehead. And the crumpled face, so hard, my God, as if he were made of stone, that sweet boy who loved me so much, and I wasn't there when he died not having had time to learn how to die."

I set the little glass down on the table and went over to the window. The park was assuming its nocturnal shape, the lights were going on, fast traffic went glittering past, the Andes were blanketed with fog and the Virgin's image hung above the eucalyptus in the dark. That's how things were for several weeks. Someday I would like to figure out why she remained impassive when the planes came flying over Santiago and swooped down to drop their rockets. I found myself watching the hill and waiting for a miracle—yes, literally. But the image seemed to avoid my gaze. Whatever it meant escaped me.

The voice was very dejected, without breaking, perhaps it would never break again.

"They came to get Cristián at dawn. Father didn't object. It didn't occur to him there might be any danger. In fact, we all thought they would ask him questions about the pictures and let him go. Luz María first went to the police, then came and picked me up and we went to check with the newspapers, the hospitals and the Ministry of Defense. The 17th my father got a phone call from a doctor friend of his. I don't know just what he told my father, but I think he already knew Cristián's body was in the morgue. The old man went and looked through about a hundred bodies on the floor in the corridor. He found Cristián and then spent the rest of the day cutting red tape so they would release the body. I think the old man was broken, even though he won't say so, and there must be some twisted joke in his defending the Junta with his mouth, while his eyes say he's torn apart forever inside. He was very fond of Cristián. They loved each other even though they didn't understand each other. I also think Cristián knew what was coming and didn't avoid it. He had set dates for all kinds of things. He was trying to reconcile his strong Catholic faith (maybe there's a stronger word) with a direct quest for God in every human contact. Not the image of God but the individual gods he found burnt out and had to rekindle. I don't think Cristián ever knew he was dying; the fact of death didn't bother him. He knew something was going to come to an end when he came back to Chile. All you have to do is read his letters or his notebook. He died from the inside out, like so many others these days; he dove into the bullets. Why did they have to kill him? This is the most common question since September 1973. What has been gained by killing Cristián? This is something else. He has gained a lot because dead men like him never stop dying; and they never stop shooting them at dawn, over and over, in slow motion, they shoot him and he gets on his feet, climbs back on the truck, he rises and climbs back on the truck and returns to the Towers, going inside and on up to the apartment and back to bed and my father weeps as he sees him sleeping, and as he sleeps a widow on the first floor denounces him, she turns in his name, the soldiers arrive and take him down in the elevator, they take him down and out to the truck, they get in the truck and drive for a while, then they stop along the road and execute him with automatic rifles, they machinegun him and steal everything in his pockets, they steal everything in his pockets and put another bullet in his forehead, they shoot him in the forehead and Cristián stands up and walks away. That sequence goes on forever. Cristián wrote in his notebook: 'The military will never be able to restrain what it has unleashed today.' They made the dead walk. How could they stop them?"

What are you all going to do now? How do your voices sound? Yours is sad, but it also sounds cunning and bold. No more tea, thank you, and no more shots of pisco, thanks, nor any more of your tears, if you'll be so kind. It's enough for me to know that I heard your voice and that you were alone, on your knees, kissing your son's bloody corpse, that you went to get a coffin and came back with the undertakers and accidentally went in the wrong room and saw a stack of bodies and they gave you the corpse of a young girl. But—such is life—the errors are corrected. And you finally left with your brother's body although you refused to look at it and I agree that cremation is probably the best thing.

I never got to see him, and I don't know what we're made of, although certain things are clear now that weren't a few weeks ago. For example, I accept that Cristián knew his death was coming and took certain precautions, some rather subtle but which suddenly mean a lot to me, since we were able to get together without much trouble and no need for explanations. We had more than two months of surprising mutual understanding; there is no other way to describe what was happening, because he was never curious about what I was doing or why, and I didn't try to convince him of anything. Cristián was a mounted angel, who rode up and down the streets of Santiago carrying a cross, collecting photographs of those who fell or escaped or died, saving some graphic proof for an editorial room in another world. As if God made him His war correspondent. Now I know why he was never a militant and why they killed him. There was never any party for him. He lived out our final unraveling. He never mentioned this, but it's obvious. On the street, Cristián captured the real meaning of what happened. Those men in uniform or those civilians armed to the teeth who talked in terms of death quotas, who later were convinced such quotas couldn't work. When you kill a man on the street, in the Stadium, or in a concentration camp or a hospital, you automatically have twenty families who enroll on your death list: passive or active enemies who won't have pity on you someday. The gospel says it: *One man died and the family of the deceased grew throughout the world and multiplied the crosses, the years and the centuries.* I told you I don't know what we're made of, but I've seen other women at the gates of the Stadium, the morgue and the cemetery, and I'm beginning to see the connection. We're in shock one moment and mourning the next, the weeks go by and the months and we're used-up, anguished and empty, but beneath it all *he* lies there waiting—still, breathless, implacable, eternal—for the right time to leap up. Nothing interests me or moves me now except the dead man I carry inside me, who won't calm down or be reconciled, who asks silent questions when you least expect it, because sometimes he stares at me through children's eyes and I hear other men and women carrying him expectantly in the street. Soon Chile will give birth to a giant corpse. Maybe Cristián repeated the acts of the Passion and we didn't realize it. I saw him every afternoon. When he arrived in June he wasn't bringing me the children, he was making them witnesses. At five and six years old witnesses see and remember. He put them between us. The experience in Virginia was like an unwanted pregnancy. The children were born there and I gave birth here. Cristián and I strolled hand-in-hand, coasting like birds from Vitacura; his consciousness grew on the motorcycle the way mine did in the slums. His Passion was going to be a film. He gathered his apostles in Pedro de Valdivia, making us believe that we were the activists and he was the innocent fellow-traveler. He didn't want to admit he was a marked man whose time was near. We gave him minor errands. Preparations were made for his sacrifice. We decided in October he would go to Europe and I would stay at my mother's until December. I see that Cristián, according to his notebook, had other plans. September 13th Cristián and I made love on the floor, on his father's blue carpet, and later he took me home and spent the night at his brother's. That night he made out a will. On the night of the 13th of October he stood guard in one of the buildings of the San Borja Towers, surrounded by traitors, bored centurions who came to have a cup of coffee brewed by the informer. The rest of us went to sleep while he looked after us until daybreak, knowing those few hours weren't enough to learn how to die. He said his prayers and waited, watching over his sleeping father. Then he climbed onto the truck, very scared and worried, suffering in silence for the pregnant woman, for the retarded youth, for the moaning husband, the blind old man, the obscure person who asks why he too has to die. And he opened his arms when they shot him and bent his head and on the ground in front of him a bloody motorcycle appeared, shrouded in the white light of the trucks. He had no time left. He didn't say a word, ask any questions, nothing. He was always preparing himself for that moment he knew was coming, but he didn't know and he would never find out what it was like."

Not far from Pudahuel Airport there is a circle of steel and engines. The passengers come and go without ever looking back. They are alone now, in the warm breeze that sweeps off the plains. Perhaps the dense blue of the night touches Luz María, as I see her so pale and serious, her wrinkled pants, the broad jacket, holding the boys by the hand, her hair fluttering in the wind, staring directly at the airplane piercing the night with its light and its whine. We stand there gazing off at the runway and the reddish dome of Santiago's lights in the sluggish dusk. Somewhere in that sky I know I'll find a cross where my brother, whom I loved but never understood, is hanging. Luz María stands next to me. Part of the sky looks like it's on fire but its flames die down behind the poplars and become motionless clouds. The cross appears at the center and the sky is the color of water now and the air is still and red and then there is a flash of light and we see the cross is only another tree, its outlines blurred, its branches composing a body. Luz María is hardened, resolved, living for the one who never asked her for anything, who grabs her attention by his silence, making her watch for these bloody sunsets, as she responds to his name and stares through him at the runway. It's getting late. I know other people are waiting and we're a long way from the plane. The red light is turning around, going on and off. The noise of the engines' driving roar fills up the valley. All the crosses are finally extinguished.

"And then in the distance we see the column coming out of the airport and heading toward the plane. I don't know how many of them there are, men, women and children, all dark, with sacks on their shoulders, walking into the spotlight that turns them on and off as they march by below and face us and lift up their fists and go inside the plane where the darkness swallows them up. She slings her bag over her shoulder, giving us her sad smile, the baby in her arms; she says something we can't understand; she raises her fist and looks at Luz María who smiles back squeezing the boys' hands. And she understands.

"Luz María goes home in the red Austin with the children. I ride off on the motorcycle I inherited from Cristián."

This First Edition
was designed & typeset by
Robert Sibley, Abracadabra, San Francisco
& printed by Buhl Brothers Printing
New Kensington, Pennsylvania
Winter 1979